The Dark Side Of Gilead

Robert Crompton

Published in 2024 by FeedARead.com Publishing

A CIP catalogue record for this title is available from the British Library.

For
Ben and Ary

Contents

* 1 *

Vic Scanlon

Chapter 1
Retracing Old Steps

Vic Scanlon always felt strange and disconnected whenever he came back to Colinton. It wasn't very long since he had left the town but he didn't belong here any more. He was a different guy from the messed up kid he used to be.

He parked his van near the Kenwood Fields Library and walked along Queens Road towards the town centre. Most of the big old houses had gone. They had been bulldozed to make way for modern flats and houses so it wasn't easy to work out exactly where Robbo's house had been. It would have been somewhere underneath one of the new apartment blocks which were nearing completion, or where the long line of modern semis began.

There would be nobody around in the immediate area who would remember. The few remaining old houses like Robbo's were all empty and awaiting demolition and all the residents of the entire street were dispersed to make way for newcomers, shuffling the town's population around. What about Robbo himself? What had become of him? Would he still be around in some other part of the town? Still as holy as hell and flaunting his superior righteousness?

He knew what he reckoned ought to have become of Robbo but, more important, what about the girl he kept hidden away? Vic had tried to do the right thing all those years before. Tried – and been warned off. Back then it was all too easy to allow himself to be persuaded that he had been mistaken, that he had not in fact seen a girl in that junk room. But maybe he did. Yes, of course he did. He was sure of it. How could he not be sure? He had met her and so had his friend Nigel, for goodness's sake, even though it was only very briefly, and he had spoken to her and she had spoken to him. And then she was gone. But not the people who said he had not seen her, that he just imagined the whole thing and he was telling lies. They didn't go anywhere. More's the pity. They just stayed there battering him: "You're wrong. You're wrong."

Well, they were gone now at long last, so what could he say with any real certainty? That was the heart of it – did he see a real girl and not a dummy or a doll? She would be a young woman now. A little bit younger than Vic. Would she be free? Escaped, maybe, or did Robbo eventually let her go? Or what if he had taken her wherever he had moved and she was still his prisoner? Or, dare he think it, what if he had murdered her? And buried her in the garden and now she was lying underneath the foundations of those new flats?

Then something hit him that he hadn't realised before, at least he didn't think he had. He was taking it for granted that the girl he had seen was younger than him. Younger. He was eleven at the time, coming up to twelve. So she was only a kid. And that had to mean that she really was only a kid of no more than about ten. Because if what they had seen was a sex toy from the Naughty Shop, Nigel had once tried to suggest and as they had half jokingly thought, she wouldn't have looked like she was a scruffy ten-year-old kid, would she? No, of course not. And she wouldn't have spoken to him either.

He carried on towards the town centre and turned up Middleton Lane, picking up the same route he had followed more than twenty years before. When he walked through the big gates into Kenwood Park it all started to come back to him more and more clearly. Clearly enough for him to feel guilty for never having pursued the matter more rigorously to get to the truth of what was going on. But what could he have done? He was only a kid.

He fingered the teddy bear brooch amongst the loose change in his pocket. It was a small enamel brooch in the shape of a teddy bear with an inscription engraved on the back, probably the owner's initials though he couldn't make out what the letters were. He'd kept it for years and years and not handled it or even seen it for ages but he always knew it was there somewhere among the assorted screws and washers and interesting bottle tops and half unbent papers clips and other assorted bits in one of the boxes on the top shelf in his kitchen. He had intended to take it back and return it to her, for surely it was hers, and he would be her hero and he would rescue her and they would run away together and live in his grandad's old tent in a secret corner of the park. And never mind how that could possibly have worked out. For a little while she was his fantasy schoolboy crush alongside, never instead of Amy Rashid.

He kept the brooch long after the girl had vanished, or evaporated into reality, and thought that perhaps one day he would be able to produce it as evidence that he was not the scheming little liar that people said he was and give it back at last to its rightful owner. The time for that had long since gone, of course, but it seemed appropriate now to find that brooch again.

Rarely now did he ever think about events back then. There were some things which might remind him from time to time – a television drama could do it, or a fairground, or perhaps a couple of street corner preachers never preaching but standing gormlessly beside their display of tracts and magazines. What he never expected was that the thing which would at last bring it all back in a tumbling great torrent and even have him driving back to Colinton to retrace his steps of twenty years before, would be a Facebook message.

It pinged into his inbox as he was setting up for a morning's work finishing a walnut writing desk he had been commissioned to design and make. As always he ignored the message at first – most Facebook messages were from people he didn't know and simply said, "Hi there," or, "How are you?" or, "so-and-so is waving at you," but this one was from Amy Rashid. Amy? Amy Rashid? Wow! And she said, "I wonder if you are the same Vic Scanlon I knew years ago in Colinton. If so, perhaps we could chat."

Back then, if Amy had ever suggested they might have a chat his knees would have melted and he would have become a dewy-eyed gibbering wreck constantly looking over his shoulder and wondering if anyone was watching what they were doing. Amy was so… well, completely out of his league. Yes, of course they could chat and now perhaps he could remain rather more composed than he would have done when he was a teenager. She responded at once to his okay.

> Vic, I am so pleased to have found you on FB. I'm working for a vet's practice in Cheshire and often return to Colinton to visit my parents. So I pass quite close to where you are now. I wonder if I could drop by for a coffee and a chat sometime? Amy Rashid.

> Amy, a chat over coffee would be good. Vic Scanlon.

> Vic, Great! Would next Saturday suit you? Hope you don't mind but I would love to ask you about the time when you spilled the beans on something to do with Len R. Personal reasons, I'll explain when I see you. Amy Rashid.

> Amy, Ah right! The girl in the junk room, you mean? Okay then. See you next Saturday – any time after 12ish here in my workshop. Vic Scanlon.

Before setting off on his memory refresher visit he went to rummage among the boxes on the top shelf of his kitchen and, yes, the brooch was still there. Not that he would any longer be called upon to prove the truth of his story or be able to return it, but that little brooch was symbolic. It could stay in his pocket now.

So now here he was, after all this time of trying to forget about the girl in the junk room, trying to bring everything back. And with the memories came all the same old doubts, with every detail dragging a doubt behind it and the whole thing going over and over again. She looked perfectly real when he first saw her but then he thought maybe it was a big mistake, because that is what the others said when he told them and sometimes he thought they were probably right. It was so crazy that it couldn't possibly be true so perhaps he had been mistaken after all and he was just imagining things and should stop being silly and forget about it. Maybe he could have forgotten about her if he had never heard her speak – or was her voice some sort of illusion as well? Surely not. Twenty years later the denials were still playing repeatedly in his head but this time, somehow, he would get to the truth about what was going on back then. Because there had to be something going on even if it wasn't what he had supposed back then.

When it happened he didn't go spreading it all around about what he had seen. He only told a few people, those who needed to know or were part of the story anyway, of course, because maybe they could have helped her. He should have known what would happen, that the folk who needed to know, who could have done something to help, would all say that he was wrong, but he knew he was right and he had made sure the he was right. Hadn't he? And they said he shouldn't go telling tales like that but he knew it wasn't right to keep quiet.

Still they battered him into thinking he probably was wrong after all and he hadn't seen her and none of it actually happened at all. Maybe he dreamed it or else there was a very good reason why the girl was there and it was nothing to do with him. So, yes okay, maybe he did have to shut up about the whole tossing thing. He didn't even tell his grandad about her, which is what he ought to have done.

Grandad did help in a way, though, because he had a sort of saying – you know what to do, so do it – and Vic could remember hearing that and knowing to speak up without needing to ask if he should. But here he was, all these years later and the thought that keeps on and on playing repeatedly, that he couldn't get out of his head, is that he was wrong and he should forget.

He had been back to Colinton before for a few days and at first it had felt good to be walking around his old places without being surrounded by people who kept telling him that he was a loser and a thicko when really he wasn't a loser at all. He'd discovered the knack of how to read without grinding to a blurry halt and he had served an apprenticeship doing the sort of work he loved. He had been to college, yes, thick Vic had been to college for a couple of years as part of getting properly qualified as a cabinet maker. Now he was running the business which his grandad had established which is lots more than some people said he could expect. He had even taken to reading books just like his grandad always did and he'd discovered why he was right all along to think that the crazy religion his parents had dragged him up into was all complete tosh.

As he walked through Kenwood Park and across the playing fields so long after that crazy time, it all began to come back clearly to him about the girl and he knew that he should never have let people persuade him to keep quiet. He could see it all again like it was only yesterday. Every detail. How the toss could anyone ever manage to forget about a thing like that? People told him to forget, to stop thinking about it. No, it never happened, they insisted. You didn't see anyone or anything. Don't go telling tales like that. So he tried to unhappen it but now it was as if it had never gone away, like a bad cut that heals up but only so far and then stays the same forever like the long gash his grandad had on his thumb which he did on a table saw when he was an apprentice. (Grandad was never any sort of a believer, by the way. He was a super guy. The best. But Vic was supposed to stay away from him and they shouldn't have lived with him for so long before getting their own house, his mother said, because he was a wicked old man and a bad influence.)

So Vic was not wrong about the story, he knew he wasn't wrong. Except maybe, maybe, it was not quite like he thought at the time. Now it was time to go over it once more, but properly this time and get it written down, and then there would be no mistaking, and he might be able to find out for certain what had been going on back then and, so far as could be possible at this late stage, deal properly with what should have been dealt with years before.

By the time he got back to his van most of the memories had woken up and were playing and replaying is his head. He poured himself a coffee from his flask and began to relax as he sipped the hot sweet drink. Those vivid memories of old doubts began to lose their power to oppress and accuse. The whole thing was falling into sequence instead of playing over and over. Perhaps by the next day when Amy was due to visit, he would have the whole thing in order. And in the meantime he would focus on how good it will be to see Amy and how much he looked forward to seeing her.

*

Chapter 2
Telling the Story

He didn't usually come to the workshop on a Saturday morning unless he was very busy with a looming deadline. Today was different though and it wasn't because he'd taken the previous afternoon off work to go over to Colinton getting that old crazy story straight in his head. It was also because he was being a bit like a dewy-eyed teenager at the thought of Amy dropping by and he wanted to show her his new workshop. The place was already perfectly tidy – he kept it that way because he liked to be able to show customers around and let them see where their work would be done. So it was not simply to impress Amy. Not at all. Besides, like his grandad always used to say, an untidy workshop is a dangerous place.

He went to his marking out table and began to transfer some markings from a profile template to a piece of four by four oak and get it ready for turning a new leg for a battered old Jacobean dining table he was restoring. Then he told himself to stop being silly, to stop being a teenager pretending to be a grown-up. He went to put the kettle on.

The door opened and a voice called, "Hello! Can I come in?" It was Amy, as lovely as ever in a bright yellow baggy sweater, black culottes and a flowered headscarf. And behind the smiling dark eyes was the same reservedly confident Amy who could step into any role she wished. "Wow!" she said as she came inside. "What a super place you have here."

He made two mugs of coffee and then showed Amy around the workshop before going to sit in the display area where a newly finished writing desk awaiting collection was surrounded by photo boards showing some of his favourite pieces as well as some of his grandad's old photos from when he first set up the business in the old premises.

"What I was specially interested in," Amy began after she had taken a good look at all his work, "was something I understand you had found out about Len Robinson. I was hoping you'd be able to fill me in on that one."

"Right, well," Vic responded, thoughtfully stirring his coffee as if to put his thoughts into proper sequence. "At long last I can tell the tale."

So, what happened was this: Vic and Nigel, who was a friend back then, they went to Brother Robinson's house and there was a girl in the little extension at the back of the house with a window that looked out into the lean-to and not properly to the outside. It was Nigel's idea to go there even if he did say afterwards that it was Vic who was the ringleader. And, of course, the elders believed Nigel's version but only in a letting-him-off sort of way because his dad was one of the elders. They didn't really believe that Vic was clever enough to think it up on his own but it was convenient to have someone to take the blame. Like everyone said, thick Vic is as thick as a plank.

Then Brother Robinson agreed, "No harm done, eh? Might as well forget it." No harm done? Well that was a joke for a start and Vic thought it was a bit fishy really, him saying that when he usually liked getting people into trouble with the other elders. Anyway, that's the short version which he did tell to one or two others back then and once very nearly blurted out to the whole congregation until he got a beating from his dad for telling lies.

Of course, there was a lot more to it than that, so he went back to the beginning rummaging around in his memory trying to gather a few more details. It was a Wednesday afternoon while he was still on the home schooling thing that his dad insisted on trying, so he was on his own at home half-heartedly doing some lesson stuff his mother had given him before she went knocking on doors telling people the wonderful news of death and destruction at Armageddon any time soon. (This was before she had given up altogether on trying to do anything remotely educational for the learning at home lark.) Vic was still pretending to be doing the lesson thing when Nigel came round directly after real school.

"Leave that," he said dangling a key on a string in front of Vic's face. "Want to go on a snooper's hunt?"

Vic shoved his book and pens and things into the drawer (his mum wouldn't bother to check on how much he had done, she hardly ever did) and followed Nigel, not knowing where they were going except that a snooper's hunt meant they'd be nosing around somewhere they shouldn't. Like poking around the building site at Parker Whelan's where they were having a new service bay installed. Or rooting about at the council rubbish tip looking for anything they might find a use for. But this time it really was a properly shouldn't sort of place. A definitely-do-not-go-in-there place.

They marched resolutely and purposefully down Middleton Lane, past the big parish church where Nigel always used to spit over the wall or where they would even go and pee in the side doorway (because the people at that church worshipped the devil) and from there they went into Kenwood Park along the avenue at the old gatehouse. At the far side of the park, through the formal gardens and beyond the churned up playing fields where the annual funfair had recently been, a long line of old houses backed onto the fields and Vic and Nigel knew one of them quite well because it was where they used to come to be bored completely brainless at the Tuesday evening Bible study group meeting.

"Where are we going?" asked Vic, suspecting by this time precisely where they were heading. "We're not going to Brother Robinson's place, are we?"

Nigel replied with no more than a gruff, "Follow me," like he was the one who was always entitled to be in the lead. Of course he was, because his dad was an elder and Vic's dad wasn't.

Vic thought they would probably go down the passage between a couple of the houses and on to the main road like they used to do every Tuesday evening, but they veered off to the right and then instead of making like they were going to join the path along the back fences and come out near the library, they headed straight for one of the houses, the one with the neatly trimmed privet hedge and the narrow gap where there used to be a little gate which had been blocked off to stop people taking a short cut through the garden.

"But that's Brother Robinson's house," Vic protested. "We can't go in there. I mean, we can't climb over the fence."

Nigel dangled the key again. "Yes we can."

"You mean that's his key? Where did you get it?"

"My mum does his bookkeeping."

Vic was thinking, so you tag along and nick his key?

"...so she has a spare key to get into his office when he's away. Like he is now." Nigel went over the fence at the gap in the hedge, unconcerned about whether any of the neighbours might see. Meekly, Vic followed. They went down the side of the house and around to the front. And as confidently as if he had every right to be going in there, Nigel opened the door.

"But what if he's…? I mean, we can't be doing this. It's… well, it's not right," Vic whispered urgently, but he followed Nigel inside anyway. And all the time he was half expecting that Robbo – Brother Robinson – would suddenly appear and catch them. As Vic tiptoed silently along the narrow hallway Nigel walked ahead making no attempt at stealth. He threw the sitting room door open.

"Shh," hissed Vic.

"What's up?" retorted Nigel. "Nobody's going to hear us. He's miles away and he won't be back until tonight."

"No but..." He shouldn't have come. Shouldn't have, Vic kept telling himself. They were going to get into serious trouble. He knew it. But he still followed Nigel into the sitting room where they always had the Tuesday evening meetings. Only the previous evening they had been in there. And, of course, there was nothing interesting. It was just the same as it was on a Tuesday when about twelve or more crowded in there for the boring Bible study meeting. Even cold and empty it was as though you could still hear Brother Robinson droning on about wonderful this or wonderful that, or else wicked them and wicked those. Only this time instead of feeling utterly bored. Vic was terrified. He knew it wouldn't happen but he couldn't help expecting that Robbo would come through the front door at any moment.

They didn't go upstairs because to do that would have been far too scary, even for Nigel and they didn't go into his office – like he might actually be in there waiting to nab them, so they rummaged around in his living room and his kitchen. There was one room they really wanted to get into but they couldn't because it was locked. With a great big brass padlock. Why would anyone want to lock a door inside the house with a big padlock? That was weird and it was what Nigel specially wanted to see just in case it had been left unfastened.

The padlock first appeared a couple of weeks earlier and a couple of the people who were at the Tuesday evening Bible study meeting had noticed and wondered. Nigel's mother, not usually being the suspicious or nosey kind where fellow Gilead folk were concerned, had remarked on the way home, "I wonder what he keeps in there that needs a padlock to keep us all out." Vic thought he knew the answer because Nigel had already told him that he'd heard something moving in there. "I think it's a dog. He needs to make sure nobody lets it loose during the meeting." And nobody seemed to wonder why, if that was the case, he couldn't simply tell folk to be careful not to let the dog out.

That was probably why Nigel fixed on Robbo's place for their snoopers' hunt, hoping he might have left the padlock off. But he hadn't and Vic thought they never would know what it was that he kept inside that room. It was the most boring stupid snoopers' hunt you could imagine, looking round a quite ordinary place which they knew already and not finding anything in the slightest bit interesting. Nothing any more interesting than when they were there for the Bible study meetings. Pointless. Completely tossing pointless.

But Nigel hadn't given up and led the way out through the back door. Instead of going down the garden and back over the fence, they went the other way across the back of the house. Nigel reckoned they should be able to take a look into that padlocked room from the outside. But it didn't appear to have any window so they went into the ramshackle old lean-to shed which was piled up with wooden boxes and bags of compost and garden tools all stacked in a jumbled mess which you would not have expected of a professional gardener. And in the inner brick wall, the rear house wall that the lean-to leaned against, there was a window. It was fairly high up because the ground sloped to the rear of the house and you had to come down some steps to get to the outside from the back door. Nigel climbed onto a box and peered inside through the grime.

"Oh gosh! Here, Vic! Come and look!"

He scrambled onto the box, rubbed a bit of the window pane clear and looked inside. There was a girl in there in the darkness, staring at them and looking really scared. “Who are you?” Vic called to her, but she didn’t say anything. She didn’t move, she just carried on staring. “Are you all right? Do you need help?”

Of course she wasn’t all right, how could she be? Locked in there like that, it was crazy.

Nigel tugged at his arm and he almost fell off the box. “Vic! Stop it! We need to go. Come on.”

“We should get help,” Vic protested.

“Don’t be stupid. Come on! Vic! Come on! We should go.”

They dashed round to the front of the house and through the gate onto the road. They looked up and down the road to check that nobody had seen them and walked briskly away. At the corner they broke into a run and didn’t slow down until they got to the parade of shops opposite the library.

“What do you reckon?” asked Nigel at last. “I mean, do you think we really did see what we thought we saw?”

“We saw a girl in the room that he keeps locked,” answered Vic, all very matter-of-fact.

“Might not have done.”

“Might not? What do you mean, might not? We saw a girl. In the locked room. A girl locked up. Of course we saw her. How can you say we might not have done? We should go for help.”

“What if it wasn’t? I mean, what if it was… I don’t know. It was so dark in there. Could have been anything just looking like a girl. Could have been a tailor’s dummy. Or something.”

“What would Brother Robinson want with a tailor’s dummy?”

They decided in the end that they really had seen a girl in that room and that she was there for a very good reason and they shouldn't say anything about it. Because, of course, if they did they would have to admit that they had been on a snooper's hunt and they'd be in all sorts of trouble. Vic couldn't forget about it, though. It was not the sort of thing that you could shrug off in an oh-well-never-mind sort of way and stop thinking about it like not thinking about going to the shop for a loaf when you don't need to or something like that. It stays there in your head and when you're bored out of your skull at the meeting the very next day and Brother Robinson is doing a talk about throwing Jezebel out of a window and the dogs eating her – yes, tossing eating her, for goodness' sake – you can only think about that girl locked up in his junk room. And it makes you think maybe you should tell somebody.

As soon as the meeting was over he walked resolutely up to Brother Clowes who was the boss elder back then and had been for as long as anyone could remember. Vic waited for him while he filled out the meeting attendance report. Clowes finished what he was doing and tucked the report into his briefcase. Vic was ready to blurt out his story; he would have done it, really would have, but Clowes walked past him and went across to the literature desk.

Vic's resolve to do what he was sure was the right and proper thing drained away. It was like reading – he could do it but he couldn't. It's as if everything gets locked and won't move. There was definitely a girl in the junk room, definitely but he wasn't sure. There was a good reason for her to be there and there wasn't. It was yes and no at the same time. Tell about it but keep quiet. Do it and don't do it.

*

Chapter 3
Making Sure

"So how did you pluck up courage to go through with spilling the beans?" asked Amy.

Vic smiled and shook his head. "I got pretty well screwed up about it. I don't suppose I would have been able to say anything unless I had been absolutely certain, at least for a little while, that I really had seen someone in there."

There was no way round it – he had to make sure. So on Friday afternoon when his mother had set his lesson for the day and then gone off door-to-door canvassing, he slipped out of the house and headed towards Kenwood Park. From the edge of the playing fields he could see the old houses at the far side and his determination to double check held firm. Still it was firm when he came to the gap in the hedge at the back of Robinson's garden. He went over the fence and walked cautiously alongside the climbing roses, trying to keep out of sight of the neighbouring houses.

There was the same disorganised lot of clutter as a few days before in the lean-to and the same wooden box beneath the window. He climbed onto the box and peered through the window. Yes, she was still there. She was lying with her back towards the window on what looked like an old mattress. Vic stared for a short while and tapped very gently on the glass. She didn't move. He thought she must have been sleeping. He stepped down from the box and came to the doorway of the lean-to. He stood there, scarcely moving and looked from side to side. He listened. Not a sound. There was nobody about. Good. As he turned to go back to the window for another look something on the ground caught his eye. He bent and picked up a brightly coloured enamel brooch in the shape of a teddy bear. Not at all the sort of thing which Robbo would ever have had. And it was too clean to have been there very long. Pocketing the brooch he looked again through the window. She was still there sleeping. Fast asleep, motionless. Quietly, he came away.

Instead of going straight home he crossed the railway footbridge and hurried along to the far side of the small industrial estate where he arrived at his grandad's workshop. *Isherwood's Joinery – Shopfitting, Bespoke Furniture, All classes of woodwork undertaken.* Grandad was busy at his bandsaw and didn't notice Vic at first. Quietly, Vic watched as he guided several pieces of timber through the machine and placed the sawn pieces beside the planer/thicknesser. Vic loved to watch him at work, and he loved the sound of timber moving through a machine, any machine. They all made quite different sounds depending upon the type of timber, how thick it was and what the machine was. Really, it should be possible to put those sounds together to make music. The last piece went through the bandsaw and his grandad looked up and pushed his protective glasses onto his forehead.

"Oh hello, young Vic. Didn't see you come in. You ready for a mug of tea?"

It wasn't a sit-down tea break, it was a wander round the workshop break as Vic ran his hand gently over a polished table top, a finely turned spindle, a rough-sawn piece of white ash, and tried the feel of a jointer plane or a boxwood mallet in his hands. They said hardly a word until, when Vic was about to come away, his grandad said quite softly, "I hope you're not getting behind with school work."

"No, I'm okay. It's hard, though."

"Aye, well, you know it's nearly the end of the school year. And it's not too late for you to decide that you want to go back. Never mind this home-schooling malarkey. You call in at your old school and tell your head teacher you want to be back so she can sort it out for you to get into secondary school."

"Wish I could, really."

"Right then, lad," his grandad replied, "next time you're going to drop in on me, you walk on past and go see your old head teacher. And you know summat? You'll find it's a lot easier than you imagine. Do it and to buggery with them goody goody Jimmy-in-the-sky clowns. Just do it."

Vic grinned and he felt good. "Yes, Grandad, I will."

He had to run home and get there before his mother got back because he didn't want to raise any suspicions about what he had been getting up to. Now, though, he knew what he was going to do. Thank you, Grandad, you answer questions without even being asked.

There was now no doubt about it. The girl was there. And whoever she was and for whatever reason she was there, it was wrong that she was locked in that room. Even though Brother Robinson was an elder, even though he took the lead at meetings, even though he could pray long and chatty prayers as though he was on close friendly terms with the creator of the universe, it was wrong that he should have a girl locked away in his junk room and Vic had to tell someone about it. Even though they all thought Vic was a thicko who couldn't read; even though they said he needed to buck up his ideas if he was to become good enough for God to allow him to survive the coming destruction at Armageddon, he had to tell someone about that girl. And he would.

Right after the end of the Sunday meeting the following week, as soon as Brother Robinson had finished his long and boring prayer telling God how wonderful the meeting had been, Vic went up to Brother Clowes and he said, "There's something I need to tell you."

"Oh yes?" said Brother Clowes, and the words came sort of rolling down his great fat belly like a gob of spit. "Oh yes, young Victor. And what do you need to tell me?"

Even all these years later Vic could still remember feeling really screwed up inside like he was going to pee his pants and make a complete fool of himself in front of everybody including Amy Rashid who was just a little bit older than him and absolutely gorgeous. "Come on, out with it, boy," said Brother Clowes impatiently. "Oh, it's a back room thing, is? Come along then," he snapped as he wobbled off towards the dreaded back room where people would be taken to be told off by the elders, or kids would be taken to be thrashed by their parents. He ushered Vic through the door with a firm shove between the shoulders and slipped the catch on the door.

"We were at Brother Robinson's house," Vic blurted out. "Me and Nigel Clifford. We went there." Of course, Brother Clowes didn't think anything was amiss here. Why would he? Probably thought Vic was talking about the Tuesday group meeting. So he waited, and glared at him like he was saying, come on stop wasting time and get on with it.

"And there was a girl," Vic continued, and still Brother Clowes didn't get the point.

"She was in the junk room. Locked in."

And now it was a bit weird that Brother Clowes still didn't seem to think anything was amiss – as if everyone has a girl locked away in their junk room. Vic was feeling absolutely screwed up by now and he was looking up at Brother Clowes almost cowering and thinking, no don't his me, like a puppy that's been caught taking a dump on the carpet. "What on earth are you saying, boy?" demanded the slobby fat elder.

"Like I said… A girl… Locked in the… Me and Nigel, we..."

"You're not making any sense. We need to bring in the others." And off he went, back into the main hall to fetch Brother Robinson and Nigel. Vic, naturally, was nearly shitting himself and Nigel looked scared and furious at the same time. So Vic began again when prompted by the spherical elder.

"Yes, so, we saw this girl. And she was… It looked like she was locked… Well, in the… We, er, looked through the window… And there she was… I think."

Brother Robinson was looking at him. Looking straight at him and not saying anything and not moving. Stony still. And then he said, "When?" That's all. "When?"

Vic glanced across to Nigel but he looked as if he was desperately trying to think of some way to say he wasn't there. "On Wednesday last week," Vic said, "but you weren't in. And we went round the back. And we , well, looked through the window and..."

And Nigel looked like he was thinking, hey that's quite good, actually, for thick Vic. It kind of… well, the way that he said it made it seem not quite as bad after all and nobody would have any reason to suspect they actually went inside the house. "Yes, you were out," he agreed, "and we , well, sort of looked round the back. But we couldn't see you. And Vic said… well, he might have got it wrong. It looked like someone was in there. But maybe..." Then he stopped suddenly and looked like he had realised something. And at the same time Vic realised something as well – they had gone out through the back door. But they didn't have a key to that door, only the front, so they would have unlocked it from inside and then left it unlocked. If Brother Robinson put two and two together he would realise they had been inside with the spare key to the front door unless, of course, the back door lock was one of the old sort that you just pull closed to lock behind yourself without needing the key. But they never found out, at least Vic didn't, how much he knew or how much he guessed.

He gave no hint of having realised. He said, "It's funny how things can look different from how they really are, isn't it? There's a lot of clutter in there – old clothes and things that need sorting out. And it all looks a bit of a jumble. But you know, boys, you really shouldn't go poking around people's houses when there's nobody in."

At that point Nigel chipped in with, "It was Vic's idea. I didn't want to… but Vic said..." And of course, they believed him because his dad was an elder but Vic's dad wasn't.

"Well, there we are, then," said Brother Clowes. "No harm done, eh? Off you go and we'll say no more about it." And he never thought to ask how Vic might have known that the girl – if there was a girl in there – was actually locked in without going inside the house. And Brother Robinson was very keen to agree "no harm done" and get out of there before anyone could ask about any details. But he did say, as soon as they were out of earshot of Brother Clowes, "You had better watch yourselves, you two. Any more of this sort of nonsense and I can make trouble for you." And he had this nasty tone in his voice like he was really threatening trouble. So Nigel insisted once again that the whole thing had been Vic's idea.

It was the nasty threatening voice that did it for Vic. He had begun to think that maybe he had not seen a girl in that junk room after all, that he had imagined the whole thing, but once he heard Brother Robinson's vicious threat he knew that he really did have something to hide. And he knew that Nigel was no sort of a friend if he could try to pass it all off as Vic's fault.

Of course nobody said, "Come on, then, let's take a look in Brother Robinson's junk room and then we will all know that there is nothing wrong." Oh no, nobody said that. They turned on Vic and said what an evil snooping little sinner he was and how, if he didn't mend his ways at once, the avenging angels of God would be sure to slaughter him at Armageddon. And as they all knew, Armageddon was coming soon. Like very very soon, even before he was old enough to ask Amy Rashid for a date which he would never be allowed to do anyway because for one thing dating wasn't allowed unless you were actually going to get married, and for another he was a bit younger than Amy.

And there was something else – how come Nigel's mother had a key to Brother Robinson's house? Okay, she did some bookkeeping for him, but having a key? For anyone else that would be enough to get you in front of a committee of elders and be interrogated about what you get up to behind closed doors. But, of course, Bro Robinson was an elder so the rules didn't apply in quite the same way to him – he could do whatever he wanted. Who would want to have a bit of you-know-what with Bro Robbo – or with Nigel's mother for that matter? Yuk. Maybe that's why he had a girl in the junk room.

Nigel came round again a few days later, again on a Wednesday afternoon after school. He walked straight in and plonked himself down in Vic's dad's armchair. "I know what it was," he said whilst seeming to say, "I can find out these things but you can't."

And, too right, Vic would never have guessed what was coming. "What what was?" he queried.

"What what what?" mocked Nigel. "The girl. Or rather, not the girl, the one you thought you saw at Robbo's place."

"What?"

He rummaged in his school bag and pulled out a magazine. "There," he said, thrusting it at Vic. "Inside the back cover."

"Where on earth did you get this?" asked Vic.

"Never mind that. Look at it."

It was almost impossible to look at. The sort of thing you would not want to be seen looking at. He certainly wouldn't have wanted his mother or his dad to come in right then and see it. It was gross. Gross. And for an eleven-year-old boy who had never even seen a girl in her underwear, those models were… well, gross. Okay, so he might secretly dream of seeing a girl like that but… But, those photographs… And in the living room where his mum or dad could come in at any moment… No. Definitely not. "Where on earth did you get this?" he repeated.

"Look at it, will you?" Nigel retorted. "Inside the back cover."

Cautiously, he turned to the back of the magazine. It was an advert. For Cindy and Dolores. "Real feel" latex inflatable dolls. Always willing, always ready.

"That's what you saw," said Nigel. "There was no girl. It was one of those, er, doll things."

Vic pushed the magazine back at him. "Take it away. Get it out of here."

"Not likely. There's no way I want it. You do whatever you want with it. Remember – we never saw a girl in Robbo's junk room." And off he went, leaving Vic clutching the grossly embarrassing magazine and wondering what the toss he was supposed to do with it.

As soon as Nigel had gone Vic wrapped the magazine in a sheet of newspaper, placed it carefully in his book bag and slipped out of the house to walk briskly as far as the bus stops near the corner of Middleton Lane. He looked in both directions to make sure nobody could see what he was doing. He took the magazine from his bag and pushed it right down into the litter bin. Then, after another cautious look around, he hurried home.

It didn't help that a few days later at one of the meetings when the topic under discussion was demon possession, Brother Clowes had to describe carefully how to deal with demon-possessed objects. Apparently you have to burn them because, if you don't, the demons will come back to give you grief. Vic couldn't understand why burning would make any difference and although he decided you had to be a very special kind of stupid to believe that garbage, he couldn't help thinking, "But what if…?"

Never mind, though, Vic had done the right thing and Brother Robinson knew he could not keep his dirty little secret under wraps forever. They all denied it but at least Robbo would have no option but to let the girl go, and return to her family. Surely?

Then, of course, he began to wonder whether he should perhaps go and see if he could tell the girl that Robbo was going to have to let her go. So that maybe she would know that Vic was the one who had made it happen. Well, he tried to but it didn't work out quite as he had hoped. He went round there on the Monday as soon as his mother had set him his work for the afternoon and gone on her way.

As before, he climbed over the back fence and crept around the edge of the garden. He stepped up onto the box which was still beneath the high window and peered inside. She was still there. "Oh! What…?

Who…?" she called in surprise when she saw him at the window. She looked really scared.

"Don't worry," he called back. "I won't hurt you. I can help you." He tried to open the window a little so that he wouldn't have to raise his voice too much. She came to window and tried to shift the rusted-up catch. Between them, they managed to open the window just a fraction – enough to be able to talk quietly.

"It's all right," he said. "I knew you were here. I saw you a few days ago. Remember? I came to this window and looked in."

She was obviously very frightened now and Vic tried to reassure her. "I've been trying to get help. Oh, and I found something – is it yours, maybe? A brooch. A little teddy bear thing. Did you drop it out here?"

"Yes, it's mine!" she said. "Give it back! Please give it back."

"I will. I I forgot to bring it with me but I'll bring it tomorrow for you. Or the day after. As soon as I can. I promise."

She suddenly looked over her shoulder, startled, towards that door with the padlock on the other side. "Go!" she said in an urgent whisper. "Go now! He's coming!"

Vic jumped down from the box, crouched down as small as he could make himself, and silently crept back around the garden and away.

It was Friday before he got a chance to return with the teddy bear but by then the girl had gone. The junk room was completely empty and the little window with the box below it was wide open as if inviting inspection. And as if saying, "Look, there was never anything in here to be in the least concerned about."

*

Chapter 4
Reading Lessons

"That's great! Thank you so much for that," said Amy. "It's lots more than I'd expected. And it must have been so awful for you. I mean, the way they treated you as if you were… Well, you were… I remember at school how, you know when we first started there. You and me, we were the bright kids. Really were. You were. But we had a couple of really awful teachers. Bullies, they were, and there were lots of kids who sort of gave up and..." She stopped suddenly and looked as though she was getting a little flustered. Maybe thought she was speaking out of turn, being too personal about the difficulties Vic faced back then.

"But, look," she continued. "You obviously did really well for yourself. I guess making the break with that horrible religion was exactly the right thing for you."

"It certainly was," Vic replied. "Bullies, like you say. A couple of those teachers at primary school were particularly bad. But I got it at home as well. I guess I knew, though, that as soon as I could I was going to walk out of it."

It all began long before the snoopers' hunt and it was stupid. Absolutely tossing stupid. Okay, so Vic wasn't the best reader in the class – in fact he was near the bottom – but that was no reason why he should have to be taken out of school for his mother to teach him at home instead of doing the extra stuff that the school offered to get him up to standard. It might have made sense if his mother was good at teaching. But she wasn't any good at all, she didn't have a clue and neither did his dad. Home schooling, though, was starting to be the in thing back then among families in Gilead so his parents probably thought this was a way to gain a bit of prestige and avoid the dire embarrassment he would put them through when he was coming up to leaving primary school if it ever got around about the head teacher sending them a letter telling them what a brainless little twerp he was. Well, not quite like that, but that's what she meant.

His dad opened the letter, read it and tossed it across the table to his mother. "What is this?" he demanded, turning to Vic. "What is this all about? Say something! Tell me! Don't sit there saying nothing! Tell me what this is about!"

But, of course, Vic hadn't a clue what it was. It could have been a letter from the insurance company for all he knew. His dad snatched it back from his mother, banged it down in front of Vic and, jabbing at it with his marmaladey finger, said in his quiet and slow nasty voice, "What is that all about?"

Vic stared at it but it was a blurry mess with the words, "Barton Lane Primary School" floating about at the top. "Don't know," he said meekly.

His dad took the letter back and read bits of it across the breakfast things. "...Victor's reading is not up to standard... would benefit from extra tuition which we are able to offer during the Easter holiday.

This could help Victor to avoid any need to repeat year six before moving up to secondary school..."

He glared at Vic for what seemed like ages. "Not up to standard, indeed! Who does she think she is? Head teacher, eh? What does she know about anything? Of course you can read. But you know what, Victor? You know what your trouble is? You're bone idle, that's what. Too lazy to do a blind thing. Well that's all got to change. Now." One eyebrow was twitching and his stupid thin little moustache curled up at one end into a nasty vicious snarl like a Yorkshire terrier protecting its bone from a prowling cat. "Go to your room and stay up there till I call you."

Vic left his breakfast untouched and escaped to his room before his dad could decide that he needed to feel his leather belt across his arse.

They called him downstairs after a couple of hours for the verdict and sentencing. Which was this: It wasn't entirely Vic's fault; it was the school as well because they had gone soft on discipline and didn't thrash bad kids often enough or hard enough. And another bad thing about school, of course, was that it was all too easy for Vic to call in at his grandfather's place on the way home and still have time to get home before his mother and make out he'd been home for an hour.

So, no more of the wicked old so-and-so's bad influence. He knew he wasn't supposed to go there but he took no notice, not a blind bit of notice. Well, that would stop. But the main thing that was going to happen was that, no, he would not attend the extra tuition that the school was going to put on for stupid kids during the Easter holidays. Those kids were a bad influence and Vic was best out of it. In fact, he was best out of it altogether and from then onwards his mother was going be teaching him at home. And, no, he was not going to move up to the secondary school where they teach kids about terrible things like evolution and false science and they turn people into wicked atheists before they even know it. Vic was going to buck up his ideas and he was going to be a good reader. He wasn't going to be left behind and have kids like young Nigel Clifford doing Bible readings at the Hall already and showing them up. No, Vic was going to catch up and before September he was going to be doing Bible readings as well and was going to be every bit as good as or even better than the young Clifford boy.

What they perhaps should have realised, of course, was that with his dad being at work all day and his mother on "pathfinder" work, being out every afternoon until five knocking on doors proclaiming the good news of impending death and destruction at Armageddon, it was always going to be easy for Vic to slip out unnoticed to call on his grandfather. Keeping him away from school would not make any difference.

The major problem with the idea, though, was that Vic's mother was a lousy teacher. Which his dad, naturally, could not possibly have known – after all, she was a fine Christian lady who believed all the right things so she was bound to be a far better teacher than all those terrible unbelievers at school. She focussed, naturally, upon reading which was really quite easy. All you had to appreciate was that sentences and paragraphs were made up of words – which were of three basic types. There were nouns, verbs and connecting words. And Vic's lessons consisted of going through articles in the magazines and books from the Fellowship of Gilead – on his own, of course, because his mother was far too busy knocking on doors telling people the good news of the Kingdom of God. And what he had to do was to take a chapter in one of the books or an article in one of the magazines and underline all the nouns in red and all the verbs in green leaving the connecting words without underlining. Easy.

He very quickly discovered that this was a big doss – because his mother hardly ever checked what he had been doing beyond glancing at it to make sure enough words had been underlined. Once in a while, though, if she didn't have to get on right away with preparing a meal or dashing off somewhere else to warn people of the coming death and destruction at Armageddon, she would make him read a paragraph or two out loud so she could check that he was making a bit of progress and demonstrating what a fine teacher she was.

It was a bit of a setback at first when she came home at the end of an afternoon and instead of the usual swift glance at his "workbook" she said, "Okay then, let's see how you've been getting on." And she picked up his book, pointed to a paragraph and said, "There, read that bit for me." It was stomach-grindingly horrible and he stumbled and stuttered, stopped and started his way through the introduction to an article about why true Christians shouldn't watch very much television.

"Okay, keep it up," she said when he'd finished and then she went to the kitchen and called to him to go and peel some carrots.

The same thing happened the following day and then again a couple of days afterwards but that third time, instead of listening to him reading in the living room, they went into the kitchen and she had him read a paragraph while she was starting to get dinner ready. And she wasn't actually listening, not properly listening. She was doing no more than simply hearing him reading something or other without paying any attention to what it was.

That helped. Weird, weird, weird. It actually helped, probably because he didn't need to be worried or self-conscious about how it was sounding. He might have been making up complete rubbish for all she knew, paying no attention. But he didn't actually have to shove a bit of rubbish in to keep it sounding like he was still reading, except just once or twice. Mostly he could simply get on with it. At least, most of the time he could.

Eventually, it all back-fired on him. His dad had been agitating for him to get up to standard to be able to do Bible readings at the Hall, expecting him to be ready for that by September after just one term of home schooling. Vic had tried hard to put it off and his mum had supported him – because she would be on trial as well, of course. So it dragged on through October and November and into December until he couldn't get out of it any longer. He had to take a deep breath and get on with it.

It was like this: on Thursday evenings they had a regular ministry training meeting and everybody was expected to be enrolled as students to do talks and readings and get "counselled" on all the things they ought to be able to do better. Vic had tried for a long time not to get dragged into that – which was one reason why he had been quite content to let people think he was a slow learner. But he couldn't dodge it forever.

Nigel had been enrolled since he was ten and was regularly doing readings and talks and Vic's dad hated to see the precocious little twerp helping his family outshine everyone else at the Hall so it was high time Vic began to catch up and show them that the Scanlons were every bit as good as the Cliffords. Then maybe his dad could get made up to elder at last, as a fine example of a good Christian head of household. After the still quite recent few weeks of being taught at home by his mother Vic ought to have been ready to make a good start with the ministry training meeting and become as well thought about as young Nigel Clifford and hopefully in due course, even better.

So there he was, ponced up in his suit and a tie like a complete dipstick, as you were supposed to be for all the meetings anyway no matter whether or not you were taking part or how old or young you were. And naturally he was feeling as nervous as mush. Nigel was there in the front row looking very smug because having already done several of these readings he was actually quite good at it. And he probably thought Vic was going to make a pig's ear of the thing. Which, of course, he did. Completely and utterly.

The trouble never was that he couldn't read. He could, but he always lacked the confidence that the way he would say the words was the way they should be said. Like "said" for instance. Vic always said "sed" and so did everybody else as far as he could tell, but he always thought maybe it should be "sayed." Mrs Dawson, the year six teacher at primary school who got the head teacher to write that nasty letter to his parents, would correct every tossing mistake anyone ever made, though she did give up on things like "said" and usually even said "sed" herself but she hated, absolutely hated people missing the "g" off the end of "-ing" words. "There's a 'g' in there," she would interrupt every tossing time. "G g g g g. Say it! Saying g g g g! Learning g g g g! Reading g g g g!"

So although Vic could actually read, he got too flustered to do it in class in case he was going to be stopped seven times through a single short sentence to repeat a word over and over until he could say it correctly. It wouldn't have been too bad if that only ever happened when reading aloud in class but he quickly learned to get as flustered about how he was thinking the words even when he was reading quietly to himself. He had regained a bit of confidence over the previous few months but he could feel it starting to drain away again. Fast, very fast.

All this was going through his head as he stood at the speaker's desk trying to brace himself to do the reading. Brother Robinson was was sitting right in front of him looking grim because he was the one whose job it was to say what the "students" had done okay and what they had done badly and how they could do better next time. He looked as if he was getting a bit impatient with Vic's hesitation but before he could say, "Go on, boy, get on with it," Vic started. Exodus chapter eight. The plague of frogs, a truly lovely story.

He rushed out the first two lines at a gallop and then hesitated. He drew in a few deep breaths and carried on. Slowly this time. Like reading a list of very unfamiliar words. Not a sentence. A list. One word. Next word. Er, another word and he wasn't doing too badly even if it did come out like he was reading a list of unconnected words that might be rearranged with a little ingenuity to make into a story. Then he got stuck on "Pharaoh" which he actually knew but it never looked right.

"Pharaoh," prompted Brother Robinson wearily.

"Pharaoh," repeated Vic and carried on with the next few words until he came to "frog" which was an easy one and he had done it already because it was in the heading before the reading actually started, but this time it looked wrong as if it shouldn't be there and anyway what he had in his head now sounded wrong. Frog, frog, frog but what if it came out as frig? Brother Robinson looked like he was thinking what a stupid little twerp this kid was.

Suddenly Vic could see clearly once more the frightened girl in Robinson's junk room. He looked steadily at Robinson for just a moment then closed his Bible and walked back to his seat without even trying to finish the reading and without looking at anyone and especially not at his dad.

Everybody was staring at him, at least he thought they were – he was looking intently at the floor in front of his feet. His mother was about to explode into a splattery mess and his father was already loosening his belt. Brother Robinson stood up. "Would somebody who is able to read like to come forward and finish the passage for us?" And, of course, it was Nigel who stepped forward.

"There now, that wasn't difficult was it, Nigel? Thank you," said Brother Robinson when he had finished. Then he got started on Vic: "Well, what can we say about your pathetic attempt to read from the Bible? The Bible – the word of God. Hmm? That was an absolute disgrace. A disgrace! You must never, ever treat your training assignments with such disdain. Next time – if we can even allow a next time – you must come thoroughly prepared. Thoroughly prepared. You understand what I mean? And look at me when I am speaking to you, boy! This was a disgrace but we'll say no more about it and trust that your father will deal with you when you get home."

Before Brother Robinson could move on with the meeting, Vic shouted out, "I saw her! I did! She was there!" He didn't see how Robbo reacted to his outburst before his father grabbed him, dragged him to the back room and walloped him hard with his belt.

Again when they got home he got another walloping, but this time a proper one with the buckle end of the belt on his bare arse. Apparently that would teach him to show a little more respect for the Word of God and for the leaders within the congregation. Well maybe it did or maybe it didn't but it certainly wasn't going to help him to read any more fluently.

Then when his father had finished with him he got it in the neck from his mother for showing her up like that when everyone knows that home schooling is far superior to school schooling and he really ought to have put on display all the benefits of her hard work in teaching him during his recent term of learning at home. Just think what a good example he could have set for all the other parents who deserve to see what fine results you get with learning at home from devoted parents. And he had to turn it all to trash in that disgraceful manner. At least they let him off having to do any more readings at the training meeting.

*

Chapter 5
Kicked Out

Early the following evening when Vic was in his room starting his homework for the weekend (real homework from real school) he heard the familiar voice of Bill Clowes downstairs. After a few minutes his dad called him to come down. His parents were sitting side by side on the settee and Clowes occupied his dad's usual chair. All three were looking very solemn and Vic knew at once that this was about his reading failure and his outburst the previous evening.

"Sit over there on the stool, will you," his dad snapped. "Brother Clowes has something important to say to you."

"Well now," the senior elder began. "That performance of yours last night. Not very clever, was it? No, indeed, you really did make a terrible mess. What do you suppose any newcomers might have thought? Someone coming to the Hall for the first time, seekers after the truth of God's Word. Hmm? And as for that dreadful outburst… No, no. Oh no, we can't have you doing that sort of thing. So here's what's going to happen. We shall not put you on reproof, there's no need for any judicial procedure. But what we'll do is have you behave as if you are on reproof. You'll keep quiet unless you are spoken to and you'll sit at the back during meetings. So as not to draw attention to yourself, you understand. And you'll go out straight after the final song and prayer.

Then you'll not be tempted to start spouting any of your dreadful nonsense. And so long as you don't make a wrong step there won't be any need for us to get you up in front of a judicial committee. Right, that's it. Off you go, back to your room while I have a chat with your father."

Vic said nothing in reply, and as he was going out of the room Clowes added, "This is for your own good you understand. You just watch your step or you'll get yourself into serious trouble."

It didn't take very long for word to get around the Hall that Vic had been caught doing something terribly bad although it was never actually announced from the platform that he was "marked" and therefore to be avoided as much as possible. Nobody was ever told what he had been doing because that would have meant saying something about the girl in Brother Robinson's junk room. So people decided for themselves what his offence must have been and mostly, as he discovered years later when he was eventually removed officially from Christian fellowship, they assumed he had been caught doing rude things with some of the fairground girls who weren't even Christians.

From then onwards he had to suffer the silent treatment, being made to sit at the back of the Hall and then go out as soon as the meetings finished and wait in the car for his mum and dad who seemed to take longer and longer after the meetings as they tried to regain a little bit of credibility for the resolutely Christian way they were treating their wayward son.

It dragged on indefinitely. If he had actually been put "on reproof" for his sins, his case would have been reviewed after a few months. But no, there was nothing official to review, just the echo of something bad which never died away. The kid who couldn't read became the weird guy who couldn't speak.

And then at last when he was seventeen and coming up to school-leaving time, he escaped. It wasn't easy but it was worth it. It was late on a Wednesday afternoon after school and he was lying on his bed staring up at the ceiling. Downstairs the phone began to ring and a few seconds later he heard his mother answer it and all he heard her say was, "Yes. I'll get him for you." Then she called to him, "Victor! Phone! You're wanted on the phone!"

It was Brother Clowes. "We need you to come to the Hall this evening to meet with some of the elders."

"Why?" asked Vic, completely puzzled about the sudden need to meet the Belief Police.

"I think you know very well what this is about. Be there at seven o'clock prompt."

But Vic didn't have a clue what it was about, although when he put the phone back on its stand his mother was standing there clasping her hands together and looking very grim and scarily righteous as if she knew exactly what was going on.

"Well?" she said before he could go back to his room.

"They want to see me tonight," he replied and he shrugged his shoulders to indicate that he didn't have a tossing clue what it was about.

"You've had it coming for a long time, so you've only got yourself to blame."

He went back to his room just as his father arrived home from work and watched the clock slowly tick the minutes away to meal time. The atmosphere around the meal table, though, was so tense that he soon lost his appetite. He got his coat, went out and spent an hour or more walking around the park before it was time to go and meet the elders. Really and truly he had absolutely no idea what was going on. Except that it was pretty obvious that he was going to be accused of some misdeed for which he could be disciplined – and not being aware of having actually done anything especially wrong he didn't have a clue how he might defend himself when they sprung it on him.

They were waiting for him when he arrived at the Hall. Brother Clowes was standing directly in front of the open door. Behind him were two others, Brother Robinson and, making up the full complement of the three wise men, was Brother Clifford, Nigel's dad. "Follow me," said Clowes and as he turned to lead the accused boy inside, the other two elders stepped aside. Vic followed the judge into the depths of the Hall and the other two came up behind as if to prevent any attempt at a getaway.

They went into the same back room where, years earlier, Vic had blurted out about the girl in Robbo's junk room but all memory of that, apart from Vic's clear guilt in the matter, had been brushed into righteous oblivion. "Take a seat," ordered Clowes, indicating an uncomfortable plastic chair which had been placed in the centre of the room. Vic did as bidden and the three wise men seated themselves in a row facing him across a long narrow table. Brother Clowes turned to Bro Clifford and asked him to open the proceedings with a prayer.

"We come before you, Heavenly Father, to ask your blessing upon all we are about to do this evening… We thank you for the privilege you have given us to be your true servants at this time of the end… pray that all who have gone astray and committed wrongdoing may be brought at last to true repentance… and pray that you will give us the strength to face up to evil and to root out all wrong from within our midst… And we thank you for the privilege of determining guilt and true repentance… we thank you and leave ourselves in your care and keeping… in Jesus' name. Amen."

Vic did not say, "Amen." He hadn't done that for ages because he thought it was all garbage.

Brother Clowes began, silently at first with an exaggerated frown and shaking his head. Then he spoke. "I think that in all fairness we should begin by giving you the opportunity, young Victor, to come clean about any wrongdoing or impure conduct you have been engaging in whether recently or in the past. Hmmm?"

Vic still hadn't a clue what this was about.

"Impure thoughts? Secret sins?" Robbo prompted.

Slowly, Vic began to realise where it was leading though it still didn't make very much sense. Impure thoughts and the "secret sin of masturbation" wouldn't normally get anyone in front of a judicial committee. You were expected to confess voluntarily and ask for help overcoming the habit, though Vic couldn't imagine anyone actually doing that. He stayed silent.

"You do realise, I hope," said Brother Clowes, beginning to sound a little exasperated at Vic's lack of cooperation, "that you are giving your parents serious concern about your spiritual welfare? Your mother has asked us to speak with you and guide you away from the secret sin that will inevitably lead to blatant wrongdoing. She tells us that on more than one occasion you have left clear signs of impure thoughts in your bedclothes." What do you say to that?"

Oh, for goodness sake, Vic thought, she goes blabbing among her idiot friends about finding a couple of wank stains on his sheets. He knew what he wanted to say but he kept quiet.

"What do you think about when you are doing it? Hmmm?" asked Robbo.

Vic folded his arms defiantly across his chest.

"You lust after Amy Rashid, don't you? Think she's, er, pretty?"

This was getting horrible. Then it got even worse.

"Think about her while you are doing it, eh? Abusing yourself. You think about the pretty young Arab girl, is that it?"

Vic was about to get up and walk out because this was so horrible but Clueless Clowes shot another one at him with, "And what about the fairground girls? We heard that you were engaged in immorality with girls from the travelling fairground last summer and probably long before that as well."

Vic had no idea at all where the fairground speculation this had come from. Yes, he liked Amy because she was nice and she was gorgeous, but the way Robbo and Clueless put it – that was vile. And yes, he was a seventeen-year-old boy so of course he had a wank now and again and sometimes didn't manage to keep it off the bedsheets, but this fairground girls thing, how did they dream that one up? It was…well, it was lies, plain lies with not even a hint of truth.

"Well?" said Clueless. "Are you going to say anything? Confess your wrongdoing and repent while there is still time. Because you know how close the end is now, and if Armageddon comes before you have left all this immorality behind, you will certainly not survive."

What lovely people they were! "Worldly" people don't even hang murderers but these fine Christians in the only true religion would have their god slaughter a teenage boy for having a wank. Robbo was nodding smugly like a stupid toy dog on a car's parcel shelf and Nigel's dad was taking notes and saying nothing. "Well?" repeated Clueless.

"No!" shouted Vic. "No, no, no! Stop it! You're crowding me!"

"Crowding you? What a silly thing to say!" Clueless responded and he said something else as well but Vic couldn't tell what it was. It was words, words words all battering at him.

He stood up. "Okay then!" he shouted. "I did it. I fucked them all and I'll keep on doing it." Then he turned his back on them and walked out and he was breathless and panting and his heart was thumping like he had run a couple of miles.

He didn't go home straight away. No way was he going to do that. He walked slowly through the town centre, up and down the side streets, out along Middleton Lane and into the park. He slouched twice around the playing fields and then around the gardens. Back across Middleton Lane and out onto the meadows and the river bank. And when at last it was starting to get dark he headed for home. He sat in the bus shelter nearly opposite home and watched and waited until eventually all the lights had been turned out and he knew his parents had gone to bed. He gave it another half hour, let himself in very quietly and, trying hard not to be heard, made himself a mug of cocoa.

In the morning he made sure not to go downstairs before his dad had gone to work and then waited until the last minute before skipping breakfast and rushing off to school while his mother was getting ready for her usual round of flogging magazines and proclaiming the good news of the Kingdom of God. And instead of going home after school he went to his grandad's place. He wanted to make sure that he was not around while his parents were at home. He wasn't going to give them the chance to demand an account of how the judicial committee encounter had gone until after their decision had been announced at the end of the meeting that evening.

It was inevitable what that announcement would be – "Victor Scanlon, being being guilty of conduct unbecoming a Christian, has been disfellowshipped, removed from the Christian congregation." There was no other realistic possibility and although nobody ever officially notified Vic himself of the precise outcome, he didn't much care. His parents would get all the gory details privately, probably from Brother Clowes, and the rest of the congregation would be left to figure out for themselves what he must have been up to. What mattered to Vic was simply that at last he was free of it.

As he sat in the living room waiting for them to get home from the meeting he knew that at least he would be spared the "what did they say?" and "what did you reply?" and "why did you not…?" and "what did they decide?" and the other whats and whys. It would be stony silence and righteous bad temper simmering below the surface. But that was okay, after all it was what he had grown up with.

It was his mother who actually spoke. Looking somewhere beyond his left shoulder to avoid eye contact, she said in most clearly righteous tones, "You must know that you will always be very welcome, more than welcome, to be here with us. Remember, this is your home and as soon as you repent and leave behind all the wicked ways you have fallen into, and as soon as you are clearly on a path leading to reinstatement within the Fellowship of Gilead you will be welcome to return." In other words, "Get out, you are not welcome here."

Which was exactly what his father said, but not until the following morning when Vic came downstairs at breakfast time no longer making any attempt to avoid confrontation. He had a bag packed already with enough to be getting along with for a few days because he knew exactly what he was going to do.

*

Chapter 6
Finding Freedom

"So you already had a plan in place for this moment?" asked Amy. "You'd worked it out beforehand?"

"Yes. Something I'd kept very quiet about all along was that whenever I had the chance I would go and see my grandad."

"And your parents didn't want you to have anything to do with him?"

"Well no, not at all. Not with Grandad being an out and out atheist. And never keeping quiet about it. Whenever we all went round to his place he would find some excuse to have a dig at religion in general and the Fellowship of Gilead in particular. Called them the holy Gillians. And he always referred to God as Jimmy-in-the-sky. Mother hated that, of course, so we stopped going round to his place and I was forbidden. I sneaked off as often as I could which would have been about once a week but nobody ever knew about it. And we hatched this plot, me and him. Grandad said I should bide my time so that when I could eventually move in at his place they wouldn't be able to force me to go back home. It meant life was on hold until I left school but as it turned out they made it all very much easier for me by disfellowshipping me when they did."

*

When it came to leaving school just a few weeks after being booted out of Gilead, Vic had to find his way as so often before past a line-up of officials and experts who all knew exactly what he wanted without having to go to the trouble of asking him. To start with, the school secretary had to fix him up with an appointment to see a Careers Advisor even though he had said umpteen times that he only needed a temporary fill-in job for a short while. His grandfather who was currently engaged on a major restoration contract was going to fix him up with a job when the restoration work was done and he would be back in his own workshop full time. But that would not be until after Christmas.

And the Careers Advisor, apparently not hearing this, said he needed to run an aptitudes test to identify the appropriate lines of work to guide him into. He spoke very off-handedly while quickly skim reading through Vic's school-leaving file. Then he spotted something which he thought did not appear correct. "What's this?" he queried. "According to what you have put on your record sheet you have four GCSEs. Maths, Geography, Combined Science and English Language. Respectable grades. But according to your head teacher's assessment your reading is not up to standard. What's going on here? Are you being truthful about your GCSE grades?"

"Yes."

"But you can't read very well. So your teacher says."

"I can read."

"Really? So why would your teacher say you can't?" He looked around his desk top and along the shelves behind him, grabbed a handful of leaflets and picked out one which he pushed over to Vic. "There, read that to me."

Vic was already a bit screwed up by the time he arrived at the office but he was completely fuzzed now so, of course, all the words and sentences got snarled up like the traffic on Warrington Road when there was a big accident. Naturally Vic could get no further than the first few words.

The advisor took the leaflet back. "Hmmm," he said, drawing it out into a long what-the-toss-have-we-got-here, hmmmmm. "Right then," he said after a few moments of pulling faces and tapping his pencil. "We'll get you on a learning needs assessment with one of our special needs people. And we'll take it from there." He picked up his phone, dialled a number and without troubling to check that it was convenient for Vic, made an appointment for him.

"You need to come back here tomorrow at eleven thirty. Tell them at reception that you have an appointment with Special Needs. And make sure you bring your GCSE results letter. We need to check those grades you claimed."

When he returned the following day he was hopeful that he might get somewhere at last and be able to talk with someone who actually understood the difficulties he had, unlike anyone previously including most of his teachers. He still felt a bit screwed up from the day before but the bloke who was to do the assessment thing was a fairly friendly and relaxed sort of guy who seemed quite happy to spend a while chatting about general stuff and he very soon got Vic talking about how much he enjoyed helping in his grandfather's workshop. And that led on to his plan to start working with his grandfather's joinery firm some time in January and then, if he was good enough, get onto a proper training program in due course.

The bloke – Vic didn't catch his name – was genuinely interested in this but brought the conversation back to the question of his reading difficulties. He had six sets of cards and Vic was supposed to take each card in a set one by one and see which was the first card that he couldn't manage to read all the way through without getting stuck. That was a really good way of getting into things – if only all official forms could be like that. Vic got all the way through each set of cards and the bloke looked at him with not quite a puzzled expression, more a sort of I-think-I-know-what's-going-on-here look. "So why have you come to us? It looks like you can read perfectly well. And you've got your career plans sorted out. So what's the problem?"

Vic could only mutter something about being slow and getting muddled and he had to try really hard not to feel completely stupid and nearly ready to cry like a baby. The bloke hadn't given up on him, though. He said, "I think I know how we can help you."

He had to go back to the waiting area and sit with two other people waiting there who both looked a bit scared – stripped of their "not got my glasses" excuses. After a few minutes the bloke came back accompanying a woman who didn't look like she was either a teacher or a careers officer. She was wearing a pair of dark blue overalls and had a pair of safety goggles pushed up onto her forehead.

"Hello," she said breezily "Vic Scanlon? I'm Lorraine Webster. Lorrie. Do you want to come with me for a chat?"

She took him along a maze of corridors, out across a yard at the back of the building, and into a workshop, a sort of teaching workshop with six work benches all of which were equipped with a basic set of woodworking tools. At the far end there was another room behind a glass partition and with a no-unauthorised-entry sign on the door. From where Vic was it appeared to be full of machines and power tools. Definitely not a learn-to-read sort of place so he was a bit uncertain at first about what was supposed to be going on.

"This is my new den," said Lorrie gesturing around the workshop. "We're busy setting up a new project in here. Did Dave tell you what we are planning to do with all this?"

"Er, no. I thought…"

"Right. What we are about is a bit of a leap in the dark but it might be something you would be interested in getting involved with. We're going to be working mainly but not exclusively with disabled and other special needs folk just coming into the jobs market. Give them a bit of a hands-on experience. A step on the way sort of thing. And our main focus will be on restoring and recycling old furniture. Other stuff as well but mainly renewal and restoration."

He glanced around the workshop and still wasn't entirely sure what this was all about.

"So you're going to be working with your grandfather but not for a few weeks yet. Why is that?"

"He's working on a contract with the restoration project after the fire at the Hexagon Gallery. That'll be finished by Christmas so he'll be back in his own place all the time then."

"Oh right. The restoration project? So it's fairly high quality work he does then? I guess that'll make him a very interesting guy to work with, but in the meantime you need something to be getting on with and maybe a bit of help with reading. Dave tells me you are a reader but you have some, er, blocks. Is that it?"

"Blocks, yes," Vic answered. "Could call it that."

"So let's see if we can help you with that," she replied and then went into the back room that Vic thought was some sort of power tools classroom. She came back with a handful of user manuals and dragging a couple of plastic chairs. She flipped through one of the manuals, opened it out at a page with lots of text as well as diagrams and handed it to Vic. "There," she said pointing to a section headed, *Basic turning between spindles*. Have a go with that." Which would have been crazy, of course, with a can't-read guy, but Vic wasn't really a can't-reader.

He shuffled to get comfortable on the chair, took a nervous breath, and started to read. "*Once the basic cuts have been mastered...*" That was as far as he got before grinding to a halt and it seemed, as so often, like everyone was crowding around him saying, "Come on, come on, thick Vic. Can't you read? Come on, get on with it."

But there were no folk crowding around, of course, except in his head. There was only Lorrie and he looked up at her and felt the tears in his eyes like a naughty puppy who couldn't help being what he was.

She was smiling and she had a lovely, beautiful big sister face and she reached out, touched his hand gently and took the user manual. "Fancy a cup of tea?"

While she put the kettle on and got the tea things ready Vic deep-breathed the tears away. "So what happens when you try to read?" Lorrie asked as she handed him a mug of tea.

"It's like listening to someone talking and someone else starts talking as well and then another and you're trying to listen to them all and you can't hear what anyone is saying. Reading is like that." He surprised himself with that answer because he hadn't thought about it that way before.

"And who are all the people talking at you when you are trying to read?"

"My teacher. My father. Brother Robinson. Nigel, my friend. Well, he was my friend once but... My mother as well. Took me out of school for a year. Supposed to teach me at home but couldn't be bothered. Lots of others."

"We'll have to shut them out, then," said Lorrie. Find you some place where they can't come. Where would that be?"

He thought she was probably going to get him to imagine being in his own room away from everyone else but he beckoned towards the power tools room.

"Oh. Right-oh, then. Lets take our chairs and our drinks in there."

Vic went straight over to the lathe. Apart from the fact that it was the lathe manual he had been trying to read from, he always enjoyed watching his grandfather working on his lathe and was starting to do a little bit of turning himself. With Grandad's help

"Tell you what," said Lorrie, "why don't we tell all those intruders to go away before we try anything else?"

So they stood together at the power tools door, the door with the No Entry sign. "Okay, after you" said Lorrie.

Vic grinned, took a deep breath and shouted, "Fuck off, all of you!"

"Yes," echoed Lorrie, "Fuck off! You aren't allowed in here."

"Okay?"

"Okay." He went back to the lathe and found the place in the instruction manual. He took a deep breath. "Here goes, then – *Once the basic cuts have been mastered you are ready to turn out finished work. The first step is ... and make each deep enough so that there will be enough wood left underneath the cut for the finishing process.*"

"Wow!" said Lorrie. "That was great."

It was the very first time that he had ever been able to read fluently while someone else was listening so closely to him.

"Know what I think?" said Lorrie. "It's not any sort of literacy problem. It's something else altogether. It's more like a sort of stage fright. Tell you what I think we should do – I've got some books in my office, easy readers. No, wait, they're probably not at all appropriate. What have you got at home? Books, magazines, whatever?

"My grandad has lots of books. Some really interesting stuff but I was never allowed to touch any of them when I was a kid."

"Do you think he would lend you anything now?"

"Oh, it wasn't Grandad, it was..." There was a memory coming back to him – and it was a memory. Really was, even though he used to think it had to be some sort of forgotten dream. It was when he was small, long before he started school and they all lived with Grandad. And Grandad used to read him stories even though his mother hated him doing that. There was one book with stories about a mongoose called Ricky who was a sort of ferrety little animal, and Vic loved that one but they had to read it in secret. And there was another time when Vic was trying to read on his own and it was a big fat heavy book with chapters about people who lived long ago and had all sorts of strange and interesting ideas. And his mother caught him reading it and she snatched it from him and told him off and then shoved the book at Grandad and told him off as well. And that was all before they got their own house and before Vic started school.

"That would come back to me sometimes," he told Lorrie. "Not often and it always seemed like a jumbled up dream. Like when it fades away and all you know is that you were dreaming about something but you don't know what. Well, it's all suddenly come back and it wasn't a dream. It wasn't. It was real."

Lorrie was smiling and looking at him like he had just told her something amazing. "Look," she said, "why don't you take a look among your grandfather's books and just read whatever takes your fancy and then you can come to my office or maybe here at the workshop might be better and tell me about what you've been reading. Maybe read a passage – we can always tell those trouble-makers to fuck off. Or, look, better still, how about if we get you signed up as the first of our volunteers here? Then you can come and help out maybe a couple of days a week as well as doing a bit of reading practice. And I think you'll find that will help."

So that's how they did it. Every Wednesday and Thursday afternoon he would drop in to help Lorrie with a storeroom full of old furniture which they were sorting out into what was restorable and what should be dismantled for its timber. And then he would sit by the lathe or the bandsaw and read aloud some passages from *The Road to Wigan Pier* by George Orwell who was one of his grandad's favourite writers.

It felt good to spend time in Lorrie's New Life workshop because it was the sort of place he liked to be where he could chat about real stuff, interesting stuff, like he did with Grandad or his customers, people who never had anything to do with Gilead Hall or their stupid religion. And sometimes he would tell Lorrie all the crazy stories about the people at the Hall and of all the ways they tried to make you believe their rubbish ideas and never trust whatever you thought yourself.

Lorrie was the first person, apart from Grandad, who listened and understood and who never said, "No you must have got that wrong, they would never be like that." They were like that, though, and Lorrie understood and somehow, because she understood, Vic could read like he had never been able to before.

By the time the workshop project was set up and the first folk were in there getting a bit of work experience and learning to use the tools, Vic was almost okay with reading properly. Most of the time. He enjoyed working in there, especially using the machinery – the lathe and the bandsaw – and it was great to see some results with the old furniture they were restoring. Best of all, of course, was the fact that it was the perfect sort of thing to be doing while he was waiting for his grandad to be ready to take him on as a sort of pre-apprentice.

So when it came time to move on from Lorrie's New Life project he was a bit sad to think of leaving it behind. He was also glad in a way, not just because he was about to start his job with Grandad. There was also another reason and it wasn't easy to say it properly because it sounded mean, but he didn't really want to be with all those "slow learners" who were now joining the project. Yes he knew that in a way he was one of them himself but he'd had too long thinking of himself that way.

"See, people have always told me – drummed it into me – that I was dim. thick Vic, they used to call me. And working here for a few weeks, well, these guys have taught me something great. I can believe in myself."

And Lorrie understood. "Well, yes," she said, "the idea is for it to be a sort of step on the way place. Somewhere to build your confidence to get you ready to move on to the next level."

*

Vic, it was great meeting you on Saturday and getting the story of your discovery in LenR's junk room. And everything else, of course, that you've been getting on with since then. Like we said, it would be good if you could come over here and I can then tell you my own story and why I'm so interested to find out all I can about LR. It's best if you come to the cottage, of course, but I thought maybe after you'd

showed me round your workshop I should
show you the Vet's place which is close by.
Love that workshop of yours btw! Amy

Amy, how about Saturday, late morning?
I'll bring choc eclairs. Vic

Vic, eclairs on Saturday, then. Amy.

He called in at the confectioners before setting off for Cheshire and suddenly realised he did not know how many eclairs and cream cakes to take. Did Amy have a partner, or children, perhaps? He didn't know. He had simply assumed that she was on her own like him. And as he wondered how he might respond if he should come face to face with her partner, he started to feel a little flustered. Had he really been letting himself imagine there could be any more in all this than the simple need to follow up a story from years ago? As he let that thought come to mind he realised that he might have let slip the previous weekend about his teenage crush on her. The crush that was still hovering around.

Stop it, Vic, he told himself. Stop it. Six eclairs should be plenty. He settled himself back into his van and headed towards the motorway.

He had imagined Amy living in very grand surroundings. In a fine sandstone house on some Cheshire aristocrat's estate, perhaps, but Bollin Cottage turned out to be an ordinary detached house built in the red brick so typical of the county. Amy opened the door as he came up the path. "Hi. Good to see you again. Come on in, I've got the kettle on."

He handed her the bag of eclairs.

"Ooh, super. That's great." She led the way into the small kitchen and began sorting out cups and plates. "You must be wondering," she began as she poured the coffee, "how I came to know anything at all about you having tried to blow the whistle on Len Robinson."

"Well I assumed it had found its way in amongst the gossips and rumour spinners."

She handed him a mug and they went through from the kitchen into the cosy little sitting room. "It was Alan Clifford," she said. "He told me about it."

"Clifford? Nigel Clifford's father? I would have thought he would be one of those keeping it under wraps. So how come he was the one to let slip?"

"It was when they caught up with me at last for all my misdeeds. Being female, basically."

*

*** 2 ***

Amy Rashid

Chapter 7
Disfellowshipped

Amy Rashid was unrepentantly attractive and although she knew full well how she all too easily planted impure thoughts in the minds of faithful young men of the Fellowship of Gilead, she did nothing to diminish her attractiveness. Nothing whatsoever. On top of that she was also unnaturally intelligent for a girl and flaunted her intelligence by doing well at school and also, whenever she deigned to comment at meetings, she would give eloquent comments and using big words which belittled the faithful menfolk of the congregation. As if that was not enough, at the age of nineteen she went to Liverpool University to study veterinary medicine and her parents, being spiritually very weak, did nothing at all to discourage her.

Despite all her flagrant deviation from the norms of pure Christian femininity, the wise old men of Gilead Hall did not get around to removing her from Christian fellowship until she was twenty-two and quite openly took part in various activities with direct connections to Christmas. Like when she was home for a few days in early December to make arrangements to spend some time working at Colinton Vets as part of the practical attachment element of her university course. It was at the same time that the parish church had their Christmas market and Colinton Vets had a stall in support of an animal charity. Naturally, she helped them to set up their display of goods for sale and publicity material. Doing that, apparently, raised all sorts of questions, like what might an all too attractive young female be doing flaunting herself among Christmas revellers?

Unsurprisingly she had a telephone call from Brother Clowes almost as soon as she arrived home a couple of weeks later for the vacation. They wanted her to meet with some of the elders right away, which meant Wednesday afternoon – Christmas Eve.

"You don't have to attend their judicial hearing if you don't want to," said her dad who had been very much on the edge of things for many years, for most of his time in fact as a Gileadite. "Because that's what it will be, you know. A judicial hearing."

"No, I'll play along with it," she replied. "And don't worry – I'll make them squirm." This could be fun.

And it was. It was the same three who had been at the helm for years. Clifford, Robinson and Clowes – sometimes pronounced "clues" but always quite clueless really. The room was set out in the same way that she had heard of from others who had gone through this procedure, with the three inquisitors in a row behind a table and with a chair for the condemned person a little distance away in the middle of the room. Before sitting down, Amy took the seat, moved it up to the table and sat down with her forearms resting on the table. And before Clowes could protest about this breach of protocol as he was clearly about to do, she smiled confidently and said, "Right then, shall we make a start? What did you want to ask me?"

Clowes shot a glance across to Robinson and then to Clifford but both men were looking down at their blank notepaper and giving no hint of how to handle this situation. "Er, yes, very well then. Brother Robinson, will you open with prayer, please?"

So he did, but instead of his usual interminable prayer explaining to God what was going on in case He should have missed anything important, he simply prayed, "God our Father, we ask your blessing upon the proceedings here and pray that you will help us remain firm in the face of wrongdoing and merciful in the face of true repentance if true repentance there should be. In Jesus' name, Amen."

"Now," said Amy, "what can I tell you? What do you need to know?"

"We understand..." Clowes began and faltered.

Amy resisted the temptation to say that she didn't think they understood very much at all.

"We understand that you recently attended some, er, Christmas festivities. Will you tell us about that?"

"Which?"

"Which? You mean you've been… Well, you've been doing a lot of this Christmas stuff, is that it?"

"Yes," she replied breezily. "I joined a few of the folks from Colinton Vets a couple of evenings ago when they went out for a Christmas meal together and before that there was a Christmas party at Uni before we all came home for the vacation."

"So tell us what went on."

"We had sandwiches and cakes. And we had drinks and music."

"What sort of music?" asked Clifford with the hint of an aha tone in his voice as if he was going to catch her out about having listened to Christmas carols.

"What sort? Well Roger, he's the senior partner, he brought his accordion and played us a selection of Scottish tunes."

"And Christmas carols?" suggested Robinson.

"Gosh no, not Roger. He's an atheist, a bit of a tub-thumper, but a nice guy. What about you guys, though? What sort of music do you like?"

Clifford was shuffling and spluttering and completely at a loss. Then Clowes snapped angrily, "Sister Rashid! Will you take this seriously! You were openly celebrating a pagan festival. You were playing music and drinking. And beside all that you were seen going into that church. Didn't mention that one, did you? You were seen helping them with their pagan activities. And if all of that were not a clear violation of Christian separateness, you know very well what sort of behaviour all this revelry leads to. You need to tell us here and now about any loose conduct that took place at these unchristian gatherings or afterwards in the privacy of your own homes."

"None that I am aware of. Are you disappointed?" She felt completely in control of this.

"Sister Rashid, you have always been one who would flaunt her charms. It is well known all around the congregation how you would encourage impure thoughts among your male acquaintances even from a very young age. Don't tell me that you don't enjoy leading men and boys on. So what..."

Got you, she thought and, turning to Robinson, said, "Well, I do remember how you could never keep yourself under control, Brother Robinson. You probably remember yourself how you couldn't keep your hands off me even when I was only ten. And you other two as well, you must remember how he would grab me and put his arm around my waist and pull me close and say things like, 'what a pretty little girl you are.' From when I was ten. So don't try to accuse me of anything improper because you find me attractive. And now I think this is over. We are done here." She got up and walked towards the door.

"Miss Rashid! Will you wait in the corridor there until we have decided what we must do," called Clowes.

"No I will not wait," she replied. "I am not interested in what you think. But in case you are interested in what I think, I'll tell you. You are dickheads, the three of you and I have nothing but contempt for you and your obnoxious beliefs. Bye bye."

They did not bother to inform her of their decision but she was never in any doubt about what it would be – and Clowes' substitution of "Miss" for "Sister" surely confirmed it. One of them, Robinson most likely, would have the privilege of announcing to the congregation at the very next meeting that she had been disfellowshipped, removed from Christian fellowship. The offence for which she was condemned would, as always, be stated as "conduct unbecoming a Christian," leaving it to the rumour spinners to construct a suitably salacious narrative to warrant her condemnation to slaughter at the impending Battle of Armageddon. Until then she would devote the rest of her wicked life to her studies and the care of sick animals.

Much to her surprise a couple of weeks later as she was packing her things ready to return to

University, Alan Clifford called at the house. Her first thought was to tell him she did not wish to speak with him but there was something in his manner that made her hesitate.

"First of all, Amy," he began almost sheepishly, "I want to apologise for how we behaved towards you at the committee meeting a few days ago. What I mean is, er, for how I behaved. I'm only speaking for myself here, not for the others. It was appalling and we should not have done it. I think, er, I think you helped me realise… well, something I should have realised long ago. Anyway, I've stepped down as an elder. Won't do it any more."

He was clearly struggling to remain coherent and Amy even began to feel sorry for him. Here was a guy who had suddenly come face to face with the fact that he had been a complete and utter arsehole for years. But this was preamble and she could tell that there was something else he wanted to say and would struggle with. She invited him inside and offered him a cup of tea.

Then, in the comfort of the sitting room and out of earshot of her dad, Clifford took a deep breath and began. "What you told us last week… I mean, what you said… What you said about how Len Robinson used to… how he used to treat you as young girl. It was… Well, it was… You see, we all knew what he was like. He was like that with all… With all the girls. And we never thought… We never let ourselves think there was anything wrong. It was … Well, he was like that, he was good old Uncle Len. Great with the kids. But it was inappropriate. We should have known better. But we … I suppose we brushed it aside. But it was creepy and we should have put a stop to it. So, look, I am really sorry for what you had to put up with. He was utterly wrong but we were wrong as well for letting him get away with it and I am sorry for my part in that." He breathed deeply like catching his breath after a burst of strenuous effort. He sipped his tea.

"It's good of you to come and say that," Amy replied. "I appreciate it. Thank you." But she wasn't going to say it's all right – because it wasn't.

There was more to come and, judging by his deep breaths and stifled gasps between sips of tea, this was the more important bit. To him, if not to Amy. "Do you remember Vic Scanlon?" he asked.

"Yes." What on earth did Vic have to do with any of this or anything else, for that matter?

"Yes, well we removed him as well. Two or three years back now. Like you, he hadn't actually done anything wrong. But, well he didn't fit. And didn't want to I suppose."

"Again like me, I guess," said Amy.

Clifford managed a feeble laugh at that. And then the serious bit: "The thing is, well, one time when he was a kid, eleven or twelve, he blew the whistle on Len Robinson. It was Vic and my lad, Nigel. They went poking around Len's place and they thought he had a youngster, a girl, locked up in there. Nigel was quick to back off and say they got it wrong and we made Vic keep his mouth shut as well. But, all credit to young Vic Scanlon, he blew the whistle even though it meant he got the cold shoulder treatment from everyone. So..." He shrugged his shoulders and looked desperately miserable and guilty.

It was good in one way that Clifford had come with this rambling and grovelling apology but it didn't help Amy. Not at all. She felt even more let down than ever at the thought that these supposedly good Christian leaders had known all along what sort of creep Robinson was and had done nothing at all about it. And then had the self-righteous gall to remove her from Christian fellowship. Amy, who had never done anything worse than get a little bit tipsy, was removed from fellowship by that pervy creep, Len Robinson.

When he was about to leave, Amy realised there was something she simply had to say. Not simply to let Alan Clifford know that he had not put things right with this. Difficult and commendable though it was, but also because she needed to say something about Vic.

"I remember Vic Scanlon," she said. "He was in the year behind me at school, primary school. And you know something? When Vic started school he could already read. He was one of four kids who were moved up into the next class after the starter term. And then by the time he was ten or eleven he couldn't read at all. Bullying, that's what it was. He got it at school and he got it at the Gilead Hall. There was one time when he did a reading in the ministry training meeting and he just couldn't cope. But the way that Len Robinson completely humiliated him was just awful, poor guy. And I don't suppose he escaped it at home either. But you know something? One day you are all going to regret your bullying.

"Yes, you're probably right," Clifford replied sheepishly. "But look, I apologise for my part in all of the… well, all that sort of thing. I think I should go now." He left without having finished his cup of tea.

*

"It's all a long time ago now," Amy told Vic, "and I guess I would have been content to let it all go. But then my dad messaged me, and he said to take a look for a video on YouTube from someone calling himself the Break-out Brother. I thought nothing of it then but my dad seemed to reckon it was interesting for some reason. It struck me as another run of the mill defector from Gilead. You probably know the sort of thing – born-again atheist pokes fun at people who still believe all the things he believed himself until yesterday. And bear in mind that this guy never showed his face, all strictly anonymous. Right, well in one of his videos he spoke about a culture of covering up cases of child abuse and then he said that in the congregation where he had been an elder there was an Asian woman who had accused an elder of molesting her when she was a kid. And that the same elder had once been suspected of other inappropriate behaviour with kids.

"And you reckon…? What?"

"Could have been anyone, anywhere, of course. And I wasn't really convinced that my dad was right to suspect it might have been Alan or Nigel Clifford. But let me show you something much more recent." She flipped open her laptop and went to her Facebook messenger page. "There," she said, pushing the computer towards Vic. "It looks like we are going to have a father and son duo making trouble."

*

*** 3 ***

Nigel Clifford

Chapter 8
Firm in the Faith

Nigel was determined that he would stand firm. He would not allow any temptations to weaken his resolve, but it was never going to be easy. A message alert on the phone in his pocket could so easily catch him off-guard.

> Nigel, It is a long time since we spoke together but I think about you every day and today especially. It would be so good if we could meet and chat. Dad.

> Dad, You know very well that I cannot and will not have anything whatever to do with you. How you, of all people, could have been taken in by apostate lies and turned your back upon God's Organisation is beyond me. Do not attempt to contact me again until you are ready to repent of your wrong and seek reinstatement. Nigel.

These occasional messages from his father were always hurtful but this one was particularly difficult because it arrived in his inbox on his birthday, as if in a devious attempt to trick him into an unwitting celebration of the day – which would, of course, have been a very unchristian thing to do. As soon as he saw that his reply had been delivered and seen, he blocked his father. He ought to have done that long ago when first it became clear that he was not going to respect the disfellowshipping arrangement.

Blocking was not easy, except in the sense of knowing it was the right thing to do. There could never be any question about that. And it was something of a relief to know that he could now feel free of the previously ever present possibility of an unwelcome contact from his renegade father. The other side of that coin, however, was the great sense of loss of his father's support. He had always been so proud of his son's achievements – from his first reading at the ministry training meeting to his school holiday stints as an auxiliary pathfinder working alongside other full-timers in door-to-door ministry.

Nigel was going places, he was on his way to the higher levels of leadership and confidently looked forward to becoming one of the youngest to be appointed elder and had so much anticipated the pride his father would show. But that was snatched from him all because of Clifford Senior's wilful wrongdoing. And it was wilful, entirely his father's fault, his own responsibility and blame, even though the rot set in with Amy Rashid, the faithless young woman who fancied herself as the Arab princess. Nigel was right, of course, to speak up about what he had seen but he could not have foreseen the dreadful outplaying of the sordid affair.

It was early December when everyone, so it seemed, was preparing to get caught up in the mindless preparations for Christmas revelries. Nigel was driving along Middleton Lane when he spotted someone walking in the opposite direction on the other side of the road. It was unmistakeably Amy the Arab whom he had not seen since she took herself off for the bright lights and decadence of university in

Liverpool or somewhere like that. She was with someone else, a man rather older than her, and both were carrying fairly large cardboard boxes. Nigel stopped at the side of the road a few yards further up and adjusted his rear-view mirror to try and see where they were going. But there was no sign of them. There were a few people going into the church and beyond that there were lots of people walking and sauntering along in front of the parade of shops. Amy and her companion, though, were nowhere to be seen.

He continued watching, expecting that they might emerge from one of the shops. They came empty handed at last from the church. The church, indeed! It was a good thing Nigel had spotted her. They drew level with his car, continued a short distance to where some vehicles were parked, and opened the rear doors of a small van. They took more boxes from the van, locked it up, and walked back towards the church. Nigel stepped out of his car and followed them, carefully keeping out of their sight. They went through the lych gate, up the short path and into the church though the big open front doors.

What on earth was going on? Dare he take a closer look into that dreadful demonic building? Yes, he ought to, he should find out what was happening because the elders would need to know about it. He took a deep breath and went cautiously up to the lych gate where there was a board advertising a Christmas Fair that weekend. Silently, he prayed. “God Our Father, help me and protect me from the work of the devil and his demons. Amen.” He took a deep breath. In, and out. And another. In, and out. “God Our Father, help me and protect me from the work of the devil and his demons. Amen.” Another deep breath.

"God Our Father, help me and protect me from the works of the devil and his demons. Amen. God Our Father, help me and protect me from the works of the devil and his demons. Amen. God Our Father, help me and protect me from the works of the devil and his demons. In Jesus' name. Amen."

His heart was beating rapidly and heavily as he approached the door and looked inside. All along one side of the vast cavern, between the tall columns and the wall with its stained glass windows, people were setting out small goods, cards, bric-a-brac, knitwear, books and ornaments on folding tables. And at the table nearest to where he was, Amy the Arab and her companion were setting out what looked like sundries for pets – biscuits, training treats, pet beds, rugs and suchlike. Nigel hurried away lest he should be spotted. "God Our Father, help me and protect me from the work of the devil and his demons. Amen."

He hurried back to his car and drove home. Behind the wheel he relaxed. It was such a good and fortunate thing that he had witnessed this blatant wrongdoing. Then he laughed quietly to himself when he recalled how, as a daft and adventurous boy, he would sometimes go and pee under cover of darkness in the side doorway of that church. "Wow!" he said almost aloud. "What a snooper's hunt that was today!"

As soon as he arrived home he told his father what he had seen. "Openly? And not trying to… well, not trying not to be recognised?

"Quite openly and clearly enjoying it."

"And it was actually in the church itself? Not in the building at the back?"

"In the church."

"Gosh. And this Christmas Fair, it's tomorrow isn't it? Maybe someone should take a quick look in and see if she's involved."

"Dad, she was there today. Helping to organise an event at the church. Of course she's involved. What more do you need?"

"No, nothing. You're right. I'll ring Bill Clowes."

Molly, Nigel's mother, remained perfectly silent until after they'd had their evening meal and Bill Clowes phoned to say that he would arrange for a judicial committee as soon as possible. "I hope you know what you are doing, you two," said Molly. "There's nowt wrong with being clever and there's nowt wrong with being pretty. They're both gifts from God if you ask me."

"But it's what you do with them that counts, Mum," Nigel replied.

"Yes exactly," said his Mother and Nigel was not sure what she meant. He had a feeling that maybe he should have spoken privately to his father.

It wasn't until later in the month that anything could be done. Amy Rashid had returned to Liverpool but when she came back for Christmas the elders were ready and she was removed from Christian fellowship without further delay – disfellowshipped, and all that Alan would say about it was that her attitude had made the decision a straightforward one. "And thank you, Nigel, for your information. You did your duty in this matter."

Driving home from the meeting after the decision to expel Amy had been announced, Alan said very quietly, "I hope we did the right thing there."

Nigel made no reply and neither did his mother.

People were usually quite subdued whenever someone was expelled but, as Nigel saw it, in the case of Amy the Arab it was perfectly clear that expulsion, disfellowshipping, removal from Christian fellowship was the proper course of action. There was no alternative; she had been quite clearly guilty of involvement in Christmas activities in the church. And what is more she had been less and less active at the Hall for quite a long time. But his dad was clearly unsettled by it and Nigel couldn't understand why.

On Saturday afternoon his dad asked him to accompany him on a couple of return visits to people who had shown interest in reading their literature. Nobody was at home at any of the addresses where they called so they took a stroll through Radleigh Woods. Then his dad asked about something which had probably been on his mind all day. "You remember a few years back when you and young Victor Scanlon went to Len Robinson's place one time when he was out? Can you remember what it was you saw there?"

"Oh for goodness' sake, Dad, that's ages ago. But, yes, I remember. I think I do. Rather vague now, though. I don't suppose we saw very much."

"Vic was quite certain at first that there was a girl or a young woman in there."

"Yes, but you know what he was like. Crazy imagination and as thick as a plank."

"Do you remember where the girl was?"

"Wasn't anywhere. There was no girl. But, yes, Vic, peered through a window and he reckoned there was somebody in there. But I couldn't see anyone when I looked. A pile of old junk. Why do ask? After all this time?"

"Oh, no special reason. Something someone said."

They carried on along the footpath and came out of the woods at the far end. "Do you ever wonder what became of Vic?"

"Sweeping floors in a warehouse somewhere I'd imagine. Something like that. You know what a loser he was."

"Was he though? Did you know that Vic Scanlon was able to read before he started at school?"

"Oh for goodness' sake, Dad, don't talk rubbish. Can you not remember the complete mess he made of trying to do a reading the ministry training meeting?"

"I do indeed remember that. Only too clearly."

When they got home he wrote a hurried note, tucked it into an envelope, wrote "Bill Clowes" on the front and slipped out again. All without a word.

"What's got into Dad?" Nigel asked his mother. "He's been very strange these past few days. Is it something to do with Amy the Arab?"

"I expect he'll tell you about it sooner or later."

He did try to talk about it after their evening meal but he got no further than saying that he had stepped down as an elder because he had been upset at how easily they could disfellowship someone when there was no real evidence of wrong-doing.

"No evidence?" Nigel spluttered. "But I saw her..."

"You saw her making a delivery. That's all. Besides, I've been looking into other stuff about our beliefs and the Bible and..."

Nigel stood up. "You mean you've been reading apostate literature? You've been listening to lies about God's organisation? I don't want to hear any of this."

"Okay, I'll say no more. Maybe another time you'll let me tell you..."

Nigel went to his own room.

Things developed fairly quickly after that. Nigel and his father moved wordlessly around each other until about a week later when that awkward silence needed to be broken."

"There is something I need to tell you," said Alan as they finished their evening meal. "I have continued to think and to pray – yes, to pray about it. About my place in Gilead. The fact is that I can no longer believe... Well, I can tell you about that another time if you want me to. But, look, I've reached the point where I have to disassociate myself altogether from Gilead and..."

Nigel walked out of the room and he never did hear what his father had to say about why he had reached his decision until a few years later.

Nigel reckoned there were two ways a person might go in response to a loved one's defection or removal from Christian fellowship. Some, finding the loss hard to take, may decide that they need to listen to all of the reasons that one had for their departure. It can be so very easy to justify this on the grounds that one wishes to help the loved one see reason and recover but all too often it results, not in the restoration of the erring one, but in the failure of the other. Nigel, on the other hand, was spiritually strong and was not going to fall prey to this temptation. He would set an example for others to follow. He moved out of the family home into a small flat and redoubled his efforts to qualify as an elder.

It was tough at first because his father took to pestering him for contact and so did his mother who followed her husband's course of wrongdoing. Nigel, however, recalled the commendable response of Michael Scanlon after his idiot son had been kicked out. He let it be known that the only way to persuade a delinquent of his wrong and his need for repentance was to stick resolutely to the Organisation's teaching on the matter and have no further contact with that person. And within eighteen months of Loser Vic being disfellowshipped, Michael was appointed elder. Nigel would follow his example.

To ensure that his commendable efforts to advance in the congregation did not go unnoticed, Nigel made sure to enlist the aid and support of Brother Bill Clowes. Within a few weeks of his parents' defection he called on the senior elder at his home to set out his plans and his concerns.

"You did the right thing," said Clowes after listening to Nigel's carefully thought out pitch. "The right thing. Here, let me share a scripture with you." He reached for his Bible from the shelf beside his armchair. He flipped through and easily found the desired verse as if it was one he frequently referenced. *If anyone comes to me and does not hate his father and mother and wife and children and brothers and sisters, yes, and even his own soul, he cannot be my disciple.* That's Luke fourteen, twenty-six, as I'm sure you know. And something you should know, Nigel, is that God Our Father has seen your faithful obedience. Keep it up and you will be rewarded. And you must always feel that you are able to call upon my help and, indeed, the help of all of us on the body of elders at any time. So remember whenever you are tempted to give in, because I know you were close to your father, remember: Luke fourteen, twenty-six – and give me a call."

Nigel came away from Bill Clowes home satisfied that all would work out for the good. He could see it already – within a few months he would be appointed servant in ministry and then, in due course, he would become one of the youngest to reach the rank of elder which was where he truly belonged. It was perhaps unfortunate in a way that his progress to his rightful position in the congregation should begin with his response to the wrongdoing of others. First Amy the Arab, then his father and then his mother. All within the space of a few weeks. But true discipleship was never going to be easy.

It soon became clear that there would be times when it would be very difficult indeed, and when the first very tough test happened the only surprising thing about it was that it had not happened sooner. He was quietly filling his shopping trolley in the supermarket when he looked up and found himself face to face with his mother.

"Hello, Nigel," she began and even managed a smile.

Before letting her say any more he put up his hand to his face as though fending off a wasp flying too closely. He could so easily have slipped, could so easily have said, "Hello, hi, Mum," but he stopped himself in time, looked away and walked calmly on without breaking his resolve to get things right.

He told Bill Clowes later in the week about what had happened, confident by that time that he would be well able to face such testing moments again but wanting also to be sure that people who mattered were aware of how determined he was to follow the right course.

*

Chapter 9
Moving up the Ladder

As time went on it became abundantly clear that the congregation was receiving a rich blessing for their faithfulness in rooting out sinfulness and negativity. A newly interested family of four – both parents and two young girls – who had hitherto been very indecisive and unwilling to make any commitment to Gilead, announced their wish to have a regular home Bible study and perhaps even progress towards baptism in due course. A few days later, following the Thursday evening meeting, Len Robinson took Nigel aside along with Paul Harrison, a young pathfinder who had moved into the area a couple of weeks before from Manchester, and spoke of yet another blessing for the congregation.

"We have had our eyes on you two young men for some time now," said Robinson in an almost conspiratorial manner, "and what we have decided in a meeting with the whole body of elders, is that we should recommend the two of you to the Regional Overseer for appointment as servants in ministry." He puffed out his chest and smiled broadly at them like a proud father. "There now, what do you say to that?"

Of course, they both agreed whole-heartedly to accept the responsibility. For Nigel there was one minor niggle – Harrison was a little younger than Nigel but there was no need for concern. He was noticeably less mature and nowhere near so spiritually intelligent as Nigel. It would take him a long time to make the grade for appointment as an elder. Nigel could still feel confident that he was on his way to becoming the youngest elder in the Region. And, confirming Nigel's confidence, Brother Robinson had something further to say when Paul Harrison left them.

The conspiratorial manner returned as he leaned close to Nigel and spoke very softly. "Now look, no need to wait for the RO to confirm your appointment as a servant in ministry, but there is a job we want you to take on. I'm sure you'll be up to it. It's the Baileys. We need to get them up to speed and making progress in Gilead. Weekly home Bible study and keeping their eyes on eventual baptism, you know the drill. So look, what we'll do is this – you take mum and dad and work through the *Teachings of Scripture* book. Okay? And I'll work with the girls with the *Guide for Young Christians* book."

"Okay," Nigel replied. "That's great."

"Good. And look, do your bit and we'll get you up to where you belong before you know it. Replace your father, as it were. Know what I mean?"

Looking back on this years later, he had to admit that this was the point when he ought to have heard warning bells ringing. What Robinson was proposing was not the normal way of things; families should study together. But Nigel barely noticed the irregularity because he focussed only upon the prospect of his own rise up the ladder.

A few weeks into this arrangement Nigel still did not realise that there was anything wrong. He called at the Baileys' home on a Monday evening as usual and David let him in with Marjorie hovering in the background. They went into the sitting room.

"Hope it's all right with you," said David, "the girls will join with us. Makes sense, don't you think, doing it all together as a family?"

"Yes, of course," replied Nigel, taken aback a little because Brother Robinson had not mentioned to him any possibility of a change in the arrangement. So they got on with it. It was tough, though.

"Okay, well, look," suggested Nigel, "Maybe with Jolynne and Melissa joining us it might be an idea to go back to the beginning and start going through the book from chapter one." And then he realised that neither of the girls had their own copy of the book. Silence. Nobody moved. This ought to have been easy, really easy, but it wasn't. Then Marjorie handed her copy to Melissa, motioned to her to share with her sister and moved a little closer to David.

"Look, no," said David, "I think we'll carry on from where we got to before."

Nigel shuffled uneasily in his seat. "Er, yes, okay. So I think we had finished chapter four. So, chapter five – *Jesus Christ, Unique among Men.* And, er, we'll be looking at the questions there at the chapter heading. That's, *What is Jesus' special role in the Divine Plan? Where was he before he came to earth, and where did he go after his death?* Right. So, all important questions for us to be very clear about as Christians."

He read the discussion point for the first couple of paragraphs. *"Why is it important for Christians to know about Jesus?"* He expected a response right away because David and Marjorie had both been fairly keen and eager to make progress, but they were both looking fixedly downwards staring at the book they shared. Jolynne was making no attempt to engage with the study and gazed vacantly ahead, looking at nothing. Melissa at least appeared to be paying some attention to the book.

"Thoughts anyone?" Nigel prompted. "Melissa? Why would you say that as Christian people we need to know about Jesus?"

"I wouldn't say that," she replied. "I wouldn't say it because it's too obvious to need saying." She stood up, dropped the book on the seat and walked out of the room. "This is so boring." Jolynne quickly followed her.

David moved forward as if he might follow them but Marjorie immediately placed her hand on his arm. "No, leave them, Dear." Then looking across to Nigel, she said, "It's all a little bit too much right now. I think we should maybe carry on without them."

They struggled on half-heartedly for a few paragraphs and then cut the study short. Nigel declined Marjorie's usual offer of a cup of tea and escaped into the cool evening air. It took him a lot longer than the walk home for him to work out how he might try to help the Baileys recover the enthusiasm they'd had when they first began their home Bible study.

He still had not come to any clear idea of what he might suggest when he next spoke with them so he was feeling rather churned up inside when he stepped into the Gilead Hall for the next Thursday meeting. It was easy enough to know what to say to any well established Gilead parents when their kids started playing up and being uncooperative. You discipline them. Good, hard discipline. Belt, slipper, hairbrush or a hand. But good clear discipline and make them fall in line. But the Bailey's were newcomers and Nigel didn't really feel confident enough to tell David he needed to thrash those girls and make them take the Bible study seriously.

He never got the chance to say that anyway, as it turned out, because the Baileys were not at the next meeting. Or the one after that. He thought maybe Brother Robinson would ask about them because, after all, they had been so very keen at first and he might suspect that Nigel might have done or said something to upset them or at least that he might know why they had suddenly dropped out. But Robinson said nothing.

Not to worry though. It was just two missed meetings. And that brought them round to Monday evening again and time for their next home Bible study. More than likely they would carry on as normal and the little hiccup of the previous week could be forgotten. After all, Nigel told himself, the girls were almost teenagers and it was only natural that they should be a bit bored and rebellious. Their parents had not been associated with Gilead long enough to be truly up to speed with proper Christian discipline. That would come in time.

All would be well, he kept telling himself right up until be was ringing the bell at their front door. But all was not well. David came to the door, stepped outside and pulled the door shut behind himself. Then, with his hand gently on Nigel's arm, he guided him back down the drive towards the gate as if he had plenty to say out of earshot of the rest of the family. But all he did say was, "Look, we are going to leave this. Okay? No more calls, nothing. Don't take this personally but least said, soonest mended. Okay?"

He latched the gate and waited a few moments as Nigel walked to his car. And then he went back inside.

Nobody made any mention of the fact that an apparently enthusiastic new family of four who could all have been expected to reach the point of baptism within a few months were suddenly absent. But Nigel couldn't let it go. It kept nagging at him though he didn't understand quite why.

Two months later Len Robinson left Colinton. For years and years he had been at the forefront of the local Gilead Hall and then quite suddenly he was gone without anyone, apparently, knowing beforehand that he was even thinking about it. One Thursday evening he was leading the ministry training meeting as usual and the following week Bill Clowes took charge. "temporarily," he said, "until we appoint someone take take Brother Robinson's place. Because Brother Robinson, you see, is moving out of the area. Quite a surprise for us all, yes, but there we are. He got the chance of living in a new home and he felt it was too good to miss so it has all happened very suddenly. Anyway, as I say, I will take over until we find a new Training Overseer."

Yes, thought Nigel, yes! This was it! He would be appointed elder, he would take on responsibility for the ministry training meeting. And he was not yet twenty-five. Definitely on his way up! So when Bill Clowes approached him after the meeting and asked for a quiet word in the back room, he wasn't at all surprised and went in quite buoyantly.

But it was nothing to do with Nigel's deserved and expected rise up the theocratic ladder. "We had a message a from your father," Clowes said in a hushed, almost conspiratorial voice. "He was around a few days ago trying to contact you. Not to worry, though. I've got all the details for you and I said I would pass it on. It's about your mother, you see."

"My mother?"

"Yes. She, er... Well, she died, you see, and the funeral is... Now, I've got it somewhere. Ah yes, here we are." He pulled a scrap of notepaper from his wallet and handed it to Nigel. "There you are. Wednesday next week at the crematorium. Two thirty. So you might want to go. Show your... well, essential family business, you might say. At least it's not in a church, so... Anyway, there we are. Message passed on. Sad she never made it to repentance."

He would attend the funeral but no more than that. He could slip in at the back of the crematorium without any fuss or undue contact. Enough to show that he was actually there and not ignoring it completely. But that would have to be all. There probably wouldn't be any gathering for sandwiches and tea, none of that sort of thing. After all they wouldn't have had any friends after leaving Gilead and there were no other family members, not that Nigel was aware of. There would probably only be his dad and the undertakers so it would be a quick in and out and then Nigel would be free of it and he could get on with thinking about his soon to be confirmed role as the Region's youngest elder.

They wouldn't have any friends. As soon as he formed the thought it began to hover about in his mind and it wouldn't go away. He even dreamed about it. About his dad, friendless. At least he thought that's what his rapidly vanishing dream was about. But before he could even get out of bed it had gone without trace except that he knew it had been a vivid dream.

And now it was about his own friendlessness. He used to say, they all did, that the great thing about belonging to the Fellowship of Gilead was that you knew you had friends wherever you went. You only had to step inside a Gilead Hall and you were among friends even if it was in a place far from anywhere you had ever visited before. But Nigel suddenly realised that he didn't feel as if he had friends. People assumed Paul Harrison was his friend. He was a young pathfinder and servant in ministry like Nigel and they worked together on the door-to-door work as well as working together as window cleaners to earn a living. So of course they would be friends.

But they weren't. Harrison was a dull-witted guy who could never remember a thing from one day to the next. He always had to write reminders for himself – he carried a notebook everywhere and whenever he saw or heard anything important out would come the notebook, "Let me write that down." Everything went into his stupid little notebook. Entirely unworthy of being a servant in ministry, he was. He was always going to be a nobody. Not at all in Nigel's league intellectually or spiritually. He probably wouldn't even be able to clean a window properly if Nigel hadn't shown him how. He wasn't as bad as that gormless twerp from back when they were kids. Vic Scanlon. But he belonged in the same box.

Vic Scanlon. Now why would he suddenly remember that forgettable idiot from way back? The kid who could see things that weren't there. Why on earth did Nigel appear to attract such idiots? First Vic, now Paul. Who next? Well, Paul's goofy sister, of course, but never mind about her for now.

By Sunday the horrible feeling of isolation had almost evaporated in the face of Nigel's growing conviction that he would very soon hear that he was to step up to the rank of elder and take on the role of Ministry Training Overseer. Nigel, though, was not the one whom Bill Clowes approached after the meeting. It was Paul Harrison. Nigel didn't hang around, though, to try and read his facial expression on emerging from the back room. He went home.

But he would have to face him in the morning to spend Monday cleaning windows together, and Nigel knew that Paul would be strutting and crowing and, without a word, saying all the time, "I know something you don't know." How on earth the local body of elders could choose Paul ahead of Nigel to recommend to the Regional Overseer for appointment as a new elder was completely beyond him.

That was not how it was at all, though. Paul was usually fairly communicative and if he had something to say that he wanted folk to know about, he would take the first chance to let everyone know. Or if he was unhappy about something then simply asking, "How are you, Paul? You okay?" would set him off pouring out a whole catalogue of woes. On Monday, though, he was clearly preoccupied with something but only responded to Nigel's prompting with grunts.

Obviously, thought Nigel, the previous day's back room chat with Brother Clowes must have been about some disciplinary matter. Paul had been caught out in some minor wrongdoing! That had to be it. Nigel smiled inwardly at the thought that Paul had put himself out of the running for any advancement of his privileges and status in the congregation. Leaving Nigel, of course, as clear favourite for appointment as an elder within the next few days. Yes!

He tried not to feel too smug about it, he really did. Shouldn't gloat about other people's failures but it was quite gratifying to think that Paul Smallbrain was on the way down again. Then at the end of the afternoon's work when they were packing up to drive home, Paul said, "Are you free this evening? Only I wondered if maybe you would fancy going for a drink somewhere. Maybe have a pint in the Royal Oak?"

This was completely unexpected. Completely. They never spent free time together. Paul was such a twerp that Nigel never had any desire to seek out his company but this was probably different. Something was going on and Paul evidently wanted to talk about it. Nigel needed to know. "Yes okay. I'll meet you in the Royal Oak. About seven o'clock?"

Nigel arrived several minutes early and waited by the street corner until Paul showed up. It felt as if he had ages to wait and he was beginning to think that Smallbrain was not going to come after all. But he did. He showed up at last as Nigel was beginning to think he should maybe go home. He wasn't actually late, only by a couple of minutes.

They went inside, bought drinks at the bar and took them into the vault, the small dark room off the far end of the main public lounge. Nigel said nothing, he waited for Smallbrain to say why he had suddenly decided to be friendly.

"Has Bill Clowes said anything to you recently?" he asked eventually.

Well of course he had. Hello, good morning, see you on Sunday. Has he said anything to you? What sort of stupid question was that? "Er, how do you mean? About what?"

"Right, well, he asked me yesterday after the meeting whether I knew anything about the Bailey family. Like had you told me anything, confided in me about anything you might not want to go any further."

"What? But why would he not ask me direct?"

"Well I guess he will. I got the idea that he thought there was something a bit sort of, er, a bit iffy going on. Anyway, I thought maybe you would want to know."

Nigel sipped at his beer and eyed Small across the top of his glass. This was definitely weird. Then something occurred to him. Enlightenment. He was simply asking around generally about how Nigel was regarded in the congregation. That's what it was. A sort of background check for his upcoming appointment as an elder. So after feeling rather edgy about this odd situation, he was able to quickly relax though he did not breathe a word to Paul about his expected elevation.

Paul changed the subject and set off on a ramble about the books he enjoyed reading and in particular about a novel, *A Conspiracy of Tall Men*, by Noah Hawley which he had on loan from the library.

"Why on earth would you want to read stuff like that?" Nigel responded. "Fiction, I mean. It's completely pointless, isn't it?"

"Not at all," Paul replied. "I wouldn't say so." But he quickly got the message that trying to talk about it with Nigel was completely pointless. So he tried a change of subject. And then he said, "Oh, er, I was sorry to hear about your mother, by the way."

"Yes, thanks. But she was... well, you know..." And then realising this appeared to indicate a lot more talk about him behind his back, he asked, "But how did you know? Bill Clowes didn't tell you, did he?"

"Bill? No. It was... well, um... I saw your father a few days ago. He was on his way to your flat when I bumped into him, and I knew him, of course, from regional assemblies. He hadn't realised I'd moved into this area. Don't get me wrong, I didn't get into any conversation with him. It was just that he asked me to pass the message on to save you both the embarrassment of an awkward encounter. Want another drink?"

"No, thanks. I need to be on my way. But if he asked you to... well how come it was Bill Clowes who told me. Not you?"

"I thought it would be better coming from him. He'd be able to advise you properly. So will you be going to the funeral?"

"I'll have to see about that." He stood up to leave before Paul had finished his own drink and went on his way with all sorts of things to fret about as he walked home to his lonely flat.

*

Chapter 10
Weakening

The funeral, if you could call it a proper funeral, was bleak. To start with, the crematorium sat at the top of a low hill looking out towards the fog-covered city. And it was almost deserted when Nigel arrived. There was one other car in the car park – his father's – so he parked as far away from it as he could. As he walked up to the main entrance he could see nobody around until he came underneath the big canopy where the hearse would pull in. And there, at the far end, almost hidden behind a pillar, was his father. He was looking along the main drive towards where the hearse would come from. Nigel held back and waited.

The hearse rolled slowly and silently up to the entrance and an attendant from somewhere inside the building opened the main double doors. Alan Clifford approached the top-hatted undertaker who emerged from the small black car which pulled up behind the hearse. Another man stepped out of the car and joined them – a small, grey-suited man wearing, unbelievably, the stupid white collar of a clergyman! For a moment Nigel wondered if perhaps he ought to discreetly slip away. But his horrified fascination with the depths to which his father had obviously sunk since forsaking God Our Father, drew him back in to observe the awful spectacle.

The clergyman led the way inside the crematorium with the undertaker's men wheeling the coffin behind him. Nigel followed his father at a distance as he walked unaccompanied behind the coffin. He slipped into the rear row of seats and sat down immediately to watch as the sorry procession moved slowly to the front.

Nigel could barely take in what was going on as all sorts of memories flashed through his head. Of times when things were well with his mother. Good times when she would take him as a small boy on the door-to-door work spreading the good news of the kingdom of God. And bad times like when, as an apostate, she tried to entice an improper greeting from him with a breezy, "Hello, Nigel," in the supermarket. And how that awful final chapter had begun with Nigel discovering quite by chance the blatant wrongdoing of Amy the Arab.

The minister at the lectern was starting a reading - "In my Father's house are many rooms..." Nigel wanted to get up and run out but he could not and perhaps ought not. But he was so very uncomfortable like when he had walked into that church to check what was going on. And all the events which that set in train kept circling in his head until he came to the conversation with his Father who had wanted to tell him something about Vic Scanlon.

Amy the Arab, thick Vic Scanlon and Paul Smallbrain Harrison. Here we are, Nigel thought, in life and death surrounded by losers, twerps and apostates.

Suddenly, it seemed, the minister was coming to an end. "...blessing of Our Lord Jesus Christ, the love of God and the fellowship of the Holy Spirit be with you. Amen." Music began to play quietly and the minister stepped down. Nigel stood up and was about to make a quick exit but the attendant motioned him to wait. Obediently he did as bidden.

The minister approached his Father, shook his hand – quite warmly it appeared – and the two walked side by side up the central aisle. His father saw him for the first time now as he came to the exit. He smiled and nodded and stepped outside the door. And there was nothing else for Nigel to wait for.

There was no avoiding contact now. "Hello, Nigel. I'm so glad you felt able to come." He offered his hand but Nigel hesitated momentarily before accepting the gesture whilst keeping as much distance as possible. As they shook hands his father grasped his forearm as if in lieu of a fatherly hug and before he knew what he was doing Nigel responded with a hug, a real son and father hug. They grasped each other tightly and Nigel began to sob. Real sobbing with real tears and he could see his tears leaving damp patches on his dad's shoulder.

"Dad, I am sorry. I am so very sorry. Dad, forgive me. Please forgive me. I am so sorry."

They walked slowly and silently towards the car park and when they came to Nigel's car his dad said, "It would be good if you could come home with me now. Cup of tea and a chat?"

Nigel was about to say that yes, of course he would but he stopped himself. "No, not right now. I will come tomorrow evening. I will, I promise I will."

His dad smiled and nodded. "Tomorrow's Thursday, don't forget. Meeting night."

"Yes, Yes," Nigel replied, slightly panicky because he had become a little disoriented. For an instant he thought of saying something like, "So when I show up tomorrow evening you'll know that wasn't a spur of the moment thing now. A flash in the pan," but he thought better of it and stopped himself. "Yes, but I'll make time."

They hugged briefly once more. "See you tomorrow then."

By the following day, of course, Nigel realised that it was a very rash promise to have made. He wondered, though, whether it was good to have said he would visit his dad on meeting night because if he had gone directly after the funeral it would all have been dealt with there and then. Done, finished, end of the matter. And it would have left lots of time for him to have repented already. But it was tough, essential family business which would need to be done at some stage anyway so it was a good thing he had given himself time for the regrets to form but no time to linger in his father's company. He could so easily have caved in to his inner feelings if he had gone back with him in the emotional state which his mother's funeral left him in. It was a narrow escape; he could so easily have given in to temptation.

He called at his father's place at six thirty – time for him to have finished his meal and in time to spend half an hour or maybe even a little more with his father and then have a perfect excuse to cut it short and hurry along to the meeting without having missed too much – and with the allowable excuse of essential family business he would have no cause to feel at all guilty about it.

They greeted one another rather more warily than the previous day after the funeral and Nigel followed as his dad led the way inside the place which had been his home from earliest childhood until only a couple of years ago. Nigel knew that he had to say that this could not happen again, it would have to be the final time. And he realised he ought perhaps to apologise for having said that he was sorry in case he had given the wrong impression.

How on earth, though, do you say sorry for having said sorry? He meant, of course, that was sorry about his mum's death, not for how resolutely he had shunned them for their apostasy. That was only right and proper and he could not be sorry he had done the right thing. But no, that is not at all how he had seen it the day before while he was sobbing on his dad's shoulder.

He glanced at the clock on the mantelpiece as they went into the living room. There was still time to cut this short and get to the Gilead Hall before the meeting started. He couldn't easily do that though, but nevertheless he could make sure to get there without having missed too much.

"Cup of tea?" his dad offered.

"Er, no. No thanks."

"Look, I'll cut to the chase. See, what I've been thinking since your mum died... Well, from when we knew she only had a few weeks left. Talked about it together. See, I'm going to sell up. Get rid of this place. It's far too big, especially now. Anyway, I'm putting it on the market and I'm going to take a flat in Rochdale."

It was only what Nigel would have expected if he had thought about it, It's what people do, isn't it? So he was planning to sell up and move – so what?

"Anyway I thought you should know in plenty of time because there's still lots of your stuff here. You can come and collect it whenever you want."

Nigel remained silent.

Then his dad said, "Ah yes now, something else." He went over to the sideboard and took a packet from a drawer. "Here," he said, handing it to Nigel. "Your mum specially wanted you to have this."

It was a large brown envelope and it felt as if there was a paperback book inside.

"Take your time," his dad said. "Have a read of it and maybe tell me what you think."

"Er, yes, okay I guess."

"So, now. Will you have that cuppa now?"

Nigel glanced at his watch. Five minutes to seven. "No thanks. I'll shoot off now and maybe call in to pick up my stuff some other time."

"Okay then. Good to make contact at last. Pity it had to be like this. But do read that book. And do drop by."

Nigel hurried to his car, tossed the package onto the back seat and drove away. He got to the Gilead Hall as the meeting was starting. By the time it finished he was well on the way to reorienting himself, getting back into proper focus after a couple of terribly testing days when he could so easily have given in to the temptation of inappropriate family bonding. He was very clear now that he would not give in. He would press on with his determination to serve God Our Father with integrity and be ready to take on the responsibilities of an elder without delay.

It was a couple of weeks before the appointment of a new elder was announced. At the very end of the Thursday evening meeting Brother Bill Clowes came to the lectern and before the closing song and prayer, he said, "Brothers and Sisters, I am very pleased to bring you some good news," and reading from an official letter, he announced, "On the recommendation of the local body of elders of the Colinton Fellowship of Gilead we confirm that with effect from 1st May 20-- Brother Paul Harrison has been appointed to serve as an elder."

Nigel slipped away quietly, not stopping to talk with anyone and especially not with any of the group of twerps smiling inanely as they gathered around Paul Smallbrain Harrison.

He parked as usual on the vacant ground behind his flat, gathered up his belongings – including the package his dad had given him two weeks earlier and which had lain on the back seat untouched until now. He went indoors through the dingy rear entrance, tossed everything onto the settee and put the kettle on.

Unbelievable. It was plain unbelievable that the local elders could have recommended Smallbrain to be one of their number. They had to realise, surely, what an idiot he was with his silly notebook and his storybooks from the library. So how could they...? The kettle began to boil but he switched it off and took a can of beer from the fridge instead.

When he returned to the living room he saw that the previously unopened package had shed its contents – an old greyish paperback book with a note slipped inside. He dropped himself onto the settee and flipped uninterestedly through the book. It was one of the often mentioned but no longer read classics of Gilead: *A Paradise Earth within our Lifetime.* Well there was a laugh for a start. Published nearly a hundred years before with that title? Whose lifetime? And millions of folk living way back then are still around and expecting to suddenly wake up in the

Garden of Eden and start getting younger any time soon? Bollocks!

Oops no! That's not how to think. Not at all. It's how his dad would want him to think. He really ought to avoid reading that book like they all avoid reading stuff by opponents and apostates. Even if it was written by one of the most significant modern servants of God Our Father it should be binned like all the lying apostate stuff that the people of Gilead are constantly bombarded with. He dropped it into the waste bin, downed his beer and opened another can.

He groaned as he woke the following morning and stumbled across to the bathroom. A refreshing shower failed to refresh or fully waken him. Oppressed. That's how he felt. A series of grey, heavy moments oppressed him. His mother's death. Unexpected, that was. The funeral, still running and re-running in his head. Grim. Coming face to face with his dad and breaking down. Being passed over for appointment to elder. And that twerp, Paul Smallbrain... Too much. That book, was it real? Really real? Truth in its time, or a plant by the devil to deceive the faithful?

He picked up his phone and sent a text message to Paul Small who he was supposed to be meeting for door-to-door work. Couldn't possibly face him right away. *Not well. Cnt meet c u Sun @ mtg.*

He dressed, lay on the settee and went back to sleep until the middle of the afternoon. Things were falling back into perspective before the evening when he felt at last that he could face a proper meal. He put some chips and a piece of battered cod in the oven and opened a small can of mushy peas. And then retrieved that book from the waste bin.

He was beginning to think now that maybe he should read it. He would make himself familiar with its contents and he, Nigel Clifford, would be the one who could show how the early, now superseded teachings were inevitable steps along the path to full enlightenment. He would confound the nay-sayers, like his own father, and prove once and for all how baseless were all their jibes and their objections to sound biblical teaching. He tucked in to his fish and chips and began to read that early step along the path to truth.

He had almost finished skim-reading the short book when the note which his dad had tucked inside the front cover fell to the floor.

> Nigel, do read this and let me know what you think. I first read it shortly after we had – quite improperly – disfellowshipped Amy Rashid. It finished me off completely. I cannot defend this garbage – and I cannot defend covering up wrongdoing either. But see what you think. Dad.

He tucked the note back into the book and dropped them both back into the waste bin.

*

Chapter 11
Breaking Out

It's strange how sometimes something really bad can actually help to set things properly in order. That's how it was for Nigel. On Saturday he made the most dreadfully awful mistake that he had ever made. It began with him feeling right back down in the mire and not bothering to send a message to Paul to say that he would not be working that day. He was going to take the time off and relax for one more day to recover and get positive. He got up late, had a coffee and then took a long walk into the town centre for lunch in a burger bar. Very nice. He didn't often do that but once in a while it was good.

At the end of the afternoon when he got home he once again retrieved that damned book from the waste bin. He put it on his bookshelf determined that he would read it again, and more thoroughly next time, and get very clear in his mind what he thought about it. But for now he was going to have an enjoyable evening out. On his own, of course, always on his own because really he never did have any friends. Not close friends.

If he had known at the start of the evening how it was going to turn out he might have taken a bus into Manchester or further afield. As it was, he walked down into Colinton town centre. And it all fell apart long before he had enough beer to be anywhere near drunk. He wasn't even a little bit tipsy. Just vulnerable, that's all.

He went into the Griffin got himself a pint of lager and perched on a tall stool at the bar to drink it. Though it was early the place was already starting to get busy. Two or three couples were drinking quietly, a group of half a dozen lads looked as if they were about to set out on a loud and carefree tour of the town centre bars. Three very attractive young women seemed ready to go off in different directions as they stood in a loose huddle and surveyed comings and goings.

Nigel had nearly finished his drink, his first of the evening, when one of the young women came over to him. Her skirt was well above her knees and her neckline was nowhere near her neck. She placed her empty glass on the bar and Nigel assumed she was going to suggest that he should buy her another. But she didn't. "You looking for a good time?" she asked.

"Er, well, I was... I suppose... Relaxing for the evening."

"Don't relax too much. Want to do business?"

Was this what he thought it might be? "I, er... I suppose, in a way..."

"Well, follow me then and I'll show you something good."

And he was following her out of the pub and into the street. She turned in the direction of the railway station and then suddenly waved down a taxi. It braked sharply, did a tight u-turn and stopped beside them. The girl got in and Nigel followed closely.

"Maureen's," she said to the driver. No more than that. "Maureen's," was all the address he needed.

They got out of the taxi no more than a few minutes drive away (Nigel paid the fare, of course) in the middle of a 1960s estate of medium-rise flats and maisonettes. It felt really uncomfortable because Nigel knew the area very well from having so often trudged along those open walkways knocking at every door preaching the good news of the Kingdom of God. The young woman led the way to the access tower and took the dismal concrete stairs to the upper level. They went along the walkway where most likely Nigel had only recently walked with his Bible in one hand and a wad of tracts in the other.

The young woman knocked at a door and walked in without waiting for a reply. "Maureen!" she called as she stepped inside.

An older woman appeared from the first door off the entrance corridor. "Hello, Angie, love. You're starting early tonight.

"Anyone up there?" Angie asked.

"No. Go on, up you go."

Nigel followed her up the stairs to a sparsely furnished bedroom.

Turning to him she said, "That's forty quid."

He hadn't reckoned on spending anything like this much, of course, but fortunately he did have the cash and more. He handed her four tenners which she stuffed into her handbag. Immediately she started to undress. For a brief moment Nigel watched her, wondering how on earth he had got himself into this situation. And then he began to undress. How do I...? What should...? Oh heck, he had never done this before and it was... He didn't know what.

She was naked on the bed, legs apart. He moved towards her. "Wait! Stop!" she said. "Condom. You need a condom. Not got one?"

What now? "Er, no, I, er..."

"That's another twenty quid. It's sixty without. And I hope you're fucking clean."

He fumbled among his clothes for his wallet and placed his last two tenners on the bedside table. Then he lowered himself onto her and cluelessly fumbled around, succeeding only with her help.

"Fucking hell," she said as they stood up to dress. "I've had schoolboys do it better than that. Don't tell me that was your first time."

He was about to admit that, yes, it was his first time but then realised he ought to keep quiet.

"It was, wasn't it! Fucking hell!"

Downstairs Maureen was waiting by the open living room door. Angie handed her a tenner. "There we go, love."

Then Maureen looked directly at Nigel. "Here, I know you, don't I?"

"I don't think so," Nigel replied.

"Yes I do. I know you. You're one of them holy Gillians what's always coming round here flogging your Bibles and books. Yes you are!"

Down on the street, when he saw which way Angie was going, he hurried along in the opposite direction before turning towards the town centre where he could find a cash machine and a very different pub than the Griffin.

He woke late and slowly the following morning. He didn't have much of a hangover because he could cope better with a large quantity of booze by now. But he couldn't cope well with the tortured dream-thoughts he'd been troubled with since his mother's funeral. As Sunday morning slowly progressed, the taunting, sneering and accusing dream-thoughts slowly morphed into waking memories of the events of the previous evening. And the dreaming taunt of an out-of-reach chance to go back and dream a different dream was gone. And the face that sneered at him was not Angie the actually quite attractive young prostitute, but Maureen who rented her bed for a tenner a time to goodness knows how many Angies and their customers. Maureen who knew where she had seen him before and who might recognise him again, if ever he set foot on that estate.

He tried to tell himself that there was nothing to worry about. Nothing about any of it would get back to the elders at the Gilead Hall. Maureen might sneer at him if ever she were to see him, but he could manage to avoid that part of town. What if someone had seen him in the Griffin though? Or getting into the taxi? Or walking across that estate? Who lived in that area? Nobody at all whom he knew. It would never get back to the elders. There was nothing to worry about. Nothing at all. Probably not. He could repent the fleeting misdeed away and it would be gone.

He washed and shaved and after a sandwich lunch he stuffed his things into his book bag and walked into town for the afternoon's meeting in the Gilead Hall. It was dull, as it usually was and unremarkable as always. And nobody said anything more than, "Hello, Nigel," or, "Good afternoon, Brother Clifford." The vague fear that Bill Clowes or one of the other elders might call him into the back room began to lift and vanished completely when Clowes, who had been conducting the meeting, called on him to give the closing prayer.

He arrived home feeling confident that he really would be able to repent his missteps away, so he went into town for a few drinks in the Royal Oak. Within a short while of arriving at the pub he realised he ought perhaps to send Paul Smallbrain a message to confirm that all was back to normal and he would meet him as usual on Monday morning for a day of window cleaning. But he did not have his phone.

Maybe he should go back home and get it because he really ought to send that message. Or perhaps it didn't matter. If Paul didn't hear from him he would assume business as usual. And as soon as he realised he need not send a message he began to wonder where his phone actually was. At home on his table? Or had he dropped it somewhere? When did he last use it? Had it maybe fallen out of his pocket in that dreadful place the previous night? Oh no, no no no. This worry was not going to go away. There was no other option, he had to hurry home and check.

It was in none of the places at home where he might normally have left it. Beginning to worry, he rang the number from his landline. It rang at the other end but it was nowhere to be heard in his flat. It stopped ringing and the recorded voice asked him to leave a message. So he waited a few seconds and tried again. Again it went through to voice mail. He had no other option than to go and find that phone – he could not risk the chance that Maureen, or whoever, might sometime answer a call coming through from any of his contacts.

He hurried down to his car feeling fairly sure that he might be able to locate the maisonette where he had gone with Angie the prostitute. Yes, he would feel utterly foolish asking whether he had dropped his phone there. But he had no option. And then, when he started his car, he saw it. It was in the small compartment beneath the radio where he always puts it when he is driving. He sent a message to Paul, pocketed his phone and hurried back to the Royal Oak for a few more drinks before closing time.

He spent all his spare time that week, warily at first and then more confidently, reading and re-reading that book, *A Paradise Earth within our Lifetime*. And there was no escaping the fact that the whole enterprise, then and now, was utterly misconceived nonsense. And it did not help when, on Thursday evening at the ministry training meeting a ten-year-old boy at the start of his own journey through Gilead, gave a Bible reading from Exodus. Not the plague of frogs which thick Vic had so memorably messed up, but the burning bush. And Nigel realised as he surely ought to have realised long before, that he simply did not believe any of it any longer.

He drove home clear-headed. The guilt and torment had lifted and he knew that he was done with it. On Saturday evening he went to the Griffin. Why not? Why shouldn't he?

He didn't arrive at the Gilead Hall on Sunday until the meeting was finishing. He lingered at the back until Bill Clowes left the platform. He approached him confidently and handed him an envelope. "It's my letter of disassociation," he said. Clowes looked at him in surprise. "Yes," said Nigel. "I'm done with it all." He turned and walked out.

But he wasn't done with it, not yet. Early on Monday evening Bill Clowes called at his flat. "Now then, Nigel," he said, holding up the letter. "This here disassociation thing. Well, look, it's all very sudden. And I don't want to say you haven't thought this through. But look, Nigel, you take this back and give it a few more days thought. And then if you still really want to go through with it, well, we'll all know it wasn't a spur of the moment thing. But before you do that, you come and talk to me maybe next week."

Disassociating was, of course,a drastic step which would have cost him all his friends and everything he had known since being a kid. So Clowes was being quite decent and, in his own way, very helpful. What Nigel didn't realise though until a couple of days later was that he had been spotted at the weekend getting into a taxi with one of the prostitutes from the Griffin, and word had already got back to Clowes about it. They disfellowshipped him before he could resubmit that disassociation letter.

What the heck did it matter, though? He would make them sorry for treating him badly – and he would enjoy himself doing so.

*

* 4 *

Amy Rashid

Chapter 12
Finding Robbo

Gilead figured hardly at all in Amy's thoughts until a until a message dropped into her inbox. "It had been sitting there for a couple of days before I saw it," she said as she handed to to Vic.

> Amy Rashid. A voice from the past here and I trust that you will remember me. You might have already seen some of the stuff that Nigel is posting as an incognito online activist but the thing is that he is about to go public with some mind-blowing revelations about cover-ups at the Gilead Hall. We really do need, if possible, for you to fill in some details about what you hinted at concerning LenR at your Judicial Cttee. I know it's a long time ago but I trust you remember. Hope you will agree to meet me some time soon. Alan Clifford.

> Alan, You are welcome to drop by sometime but I don't think there's anything I can add to what I already told you. Amy.

"And have you met him yet?" Vic asked.

"Yes. And that's what prompted me to try and get in touch with you. Because Alan was very much in the background. Nigel was the one who taking the lead in everything with Alan following meekly on. They've clearly got some crazy agenda and I don't trust them. It makes no odds to me at all whatever they accuse the Gilead Hall wackos of. But if their incognito stuff really is what my dad had pointed out to me then I suspect that when Nigel reveals who he really is he will paint me into the picture as well. As one of a group of vulnerable kids bribing a dirty old man."

Vic thought for a moment. "Hmm. I think I get the picture. And, sure, I wouldn't put it past Nigel to, well, invent something quite lurid."

"So what I need to do... But, hey, first, I have to pick up some things from the surgery. Fancy a walk?

It took only a few minutes of their pleasant half hour walk along the country lane for them to decide that two things would be needed. They had to track down Len Robinson and get whatever they could from him; and they needed, if possible, to trace the girl who had been locked in his junk room.

"Should be able to find Robinson," said Amy. "My dad will probably be able to ask around. But I don't suppose he will tell us very much."

"If he's still alive," said Vic. "How the toss do we track down the girl, though?"

"Is that even possible?" said Amy.

"Might be. We can give it a go."

"And we probably should do, before Nigel gets in on it and starts turning her story into something even worse than it was to bash Gilead with."

And that is what they did. First, according to what Omar, Amy's dad, knew Robinson had moved out of the area a few years before to somewhere in Wales – which didn't help very much, of course. Looking for jobbing gardeners named Robinson found nobody in any of the possible locations and looking for the name on Facebook found far too many, mostly without further information, to be remotely useful. After a couple of hours sitting with Amy's computer in her consulting room nothing at all looked like offering any useful leads.

"We could try asking Bill Clowes," she suggested. Obvious, really, when it's the only remaining possibility.

"Okay," replied Vic cautiously. "But how do we get beyond the double blocker of him not wanting to speak to either of us because we are disfellowshipped, and then not being willing to give personal information?"

"We'll have to resort to a bit of subterfuge. But we should be able to get it out of him somehow."

Vic didn't appear very keen on it but he went along with Amy's bold idea to get Robbo's address from Bill Clowes. He might not be too happy to give the information but they could at least try. Amy, though, was confident as together they strode up to his front door. She rang the bell. No response. She knocked loudly and listened close to the door. "Ah! Movement inside! Someone's coming."

The door opened slightly and Bill Clowes's unmistakeable face peered through the narrow opening. He looked older, much older, than she remembered him and had apparently lost a lot of weight. But he looked far from well.

"Hello, Bill," she said quite breezily. "Remember me? Amy. Amy Rashid."

He looked at her vacantly and seemed as if he did not remember her. But he must have done, surely? But what about Vic though? It was a good few years, yes, since they'd had any contact but Amy was hardly easy to forget. Vic was different. He was a perfectly ordinary decent looking sort of guy – prematurely balding but unremarkable and far away from the youth he would have been when Clowes last saw him.

"And this is..." She hesitated, thinking it might be a good idea not to jog his memory too much. "... this is my friend."

He looked from one to the other and appeared as if he might not have realised who they were.

"It's a courtesy call really," Amy began. "We need some information and I know you might prefer not to give it to us but we felt you should have the opportunity to tell us without us having to involve the authorities."

"Authorities? How do you mean?" He was much more alert now.

"Well we don't want do it that way if we can avoid it because nothing at all may come of it in the end. It's that we need an address. Len Robinson. We have to check some facts with him and then maybe we won't have to take it to the police."

"Police? What do you mean?"

"Well we can't tell you any more than that because the rumours might be completely unfounded. So if you have his address that would really help."

"Yes, yes, of course. Wait there." He shuffled away, closing the door as he left.

They waited. And waited. And began to wonder if he was ignoring them. He came back eventually and opened the door wide enough to hand Amy a slip of paper. She glanced at it briefly and showed it to Vic. "Thank you," she said. "We'll not trouble you any further."

A few days later they took the first opportunity they had to drive to Porthmadog and a just little further on to Cwm Croeswen. The valley, which was not too far away from the town, was easy enough to find. The road sloped quite steeply downwards at first for a short distance. It went round a sharp bend and there ahead of them a long-since-abandoned car was suspended between the road and the stream below, wedged firmly in place by the willow branches which had grown through its missing windows. Just beyond the remains of the car, an ivy-entangled derelict caravan was in the slow process of being swallowed by the valley.

Ty Croeswen, Robinson's place, was the only house on the short road. It looked out across the narrow road to the fields beyond the stream. Behind, the steep cliff of what might have been an old quarry towered above the few outbuildings at the rear. Amy drove carefully onto the gravelly area at the front.

"Here we are then. You ready?" She turned off the ignition and walked towards the front door, glad to have Vic beside her helping to prevent this desolate valley draining all her confidence away. She knocked loudly at the door.

Having seen Bill Clowes just a few days previously looking woefully unwell and barely able, it seemed, to keep going, she half expected to see a similar deterioration or ageing in Len Robinson. The man who came to the door, however, was perfectly fit. A little greyer, perhaps, but tanned and looking very healthy and plainly the same Len Robinson as ten years earlier.

"Good afternoon," said Amy. "Len Robinson? I'm..."

He smiled. A perfectly genuine looking smile. "Amy Rashid, aren't you? Well, well, well. This is, er, unexpected." Turning to Vic and looking him up and down, he added, "And you must be Vic, aren't you? Vic Scanlon? Come in, do come in. Would you like a cup of tea?"

Cautiously they followed him into the house. Amy shot a glance at Vic and she could read his expression right away. Crazy, this is just crazy, he was thinking. And it was. Robinson should have been furtive, nervous. He should have been backing away like a dog who doesn't like vets. Keep away from me. Keep away. But instead he was... What? He was ready for them. Clowes had obviously forewarned him and he had worked out a strategy for handling what he must have been sure they wanted.

Amy, though, was not going to give him the chance to simply bluster his way through a plain denial of the facts. She was far more subtle than that.

"What we are after..." she began when he came back into the living room with three mugs of tea, "...was, well a bit of help really."

"Help? Oh. Like, what can...?"

Had this taken him off guard already? "It's Nigel Clifford, you see. Remember Nigel who disassociated himself a few years ago?"

Warily curious, Robinson replied, "Nigel? Of course I remember him. What does...? But, look, he didn't disassociate. No, no, not at all," he said with a flicker of a smile. "They had to expel him. Disfellowship him. You see, Nigel... Yes, a very promising young brother at first. But he went off the rails. Took to visiting prostitutes. So, naturally, they disfellowshipped him. Not long after I'd moved down here."

It was Amy's turn to be taken off guard. "Oh gosh. Right. Not something he would want to boast about." This did not square at all with the rather self-laudatory way that Nigel described himself. "Oh, right. But tell me," she asked, "are you aware of his current venture?"

Robinson was hovering between confidence and caution. "Current venture? What's that?"

"He's set up a YouTube channel. Posts videos regularly attacking Gilead beliefs and practices. It's all anonymous for now, but we understand that he's planning to show his face quite soon. He styles himself: Break-out Brother; the ex-Gilead Elder who found freedom."

Robinson was shaking his head dismissively. "No, not him," he said. "Not Nigel Clifford. Never was an elder. He was a servant."

Amy was thrown off balance a little by this, but not completely. "Whoever this anonymous 'Break-out Brother' is, he quite definitely has a lot of information that points unmistakeably to Colinton's Gilead Hall. And somewhere along the way Nigel Clifford's involved. His dad as well, in the background." She shot a glance towards Vic to hand over the baton to him.

"So the other thing we need to know about is the young girl who was at your place back then when Nigel and I were kids."

"Oh for pity's sake! Are you still going on about that? There never was any girl there. Never. Okay, you might have seen somebody, sometime. There was always trouble back then with kids coming across the back. Breaking into people's sheds. It was always worse when the travelling fairground came to the park."

Vic didn't respond right away. He just looked at Robinson steadily and if Amy hadn't known what a creepy sort of guy he used to be, she could easily have thought that there was no more to the matter than what he had just said. But there was more. She was sure of it and so, quite clearly was Vic whose steady gaze for just those few seconds appeared to unsettle Robinson.

"But that particular one," said Vic, continuing to look steadily at Robinson. "The one who didn't just scarper. When you had to put a lock on the door. What became of her?"

Robinson was flustered now but he quickly regained his composure. "No, no. She was never locked in there, if that's what you're thinking. That was just to keep her out of the house. She was free to go at any time. There was another door to the outside. So I left that one open and put a lock on the inside door. She could easily..."

What was he doing? Why the sudden switch from outright denial to a sort of partial admission and explanation? A quick change from plan A to plan B? "So why didn't she? What became of her?"

"She had nowhere to go. Didn't know where she was or where she had come from. That's why I let her stay for a while. Then I got her a place in a children's care home. And if you ask me, that's what any decent person would have done."

And that was probably as much as they were likely to get from him. She cast a questioning glance in Vic's direction and thought he seemed to agree.

"Well, okay then. That's been helpful, I think. We can be on our way now."

As they were about to step outside the house, she turned to ask him one last question but Vic beat her to it.

"Which care home was that?" he asked.

"Which?"

"Yes. Which children's care home was it where you got her a place?"

"Oh, right. Yes. Goodness, it's so long ago. I forget all the details. The Nest, Cuckoo's Nest maybe or something like that? Just up the road and round the corner from some big supermarket."

"Near the Co-op, you mean? Along Middleton Road somewhere?"

"No, no. Not there. Some other place. I forget exactly where."

"Okay. Thanks."

They drove the short distance into town and parked near the harbour. "So, what do you make of all that?" said Amy.

"All probably true as far as it goes. But there is a lot more to it that he is not letting on about."

"And what about Nigel? Do we still think he is the break-out brother? Or is there there someone else as well? The ex-Gilead elder who made a brave dash for freedom?"

"It's got to be Nigel the champion bullshitter. And he pretty well told you so himself, didn't he?"

"I suppose the question now," said Amy as they walked towards Beach Coffee Shop, "is, have we come to a dead end? Hit the brick wall?"

"Probably have," said Vic. "It's a big anti-climax, though. For ages I was battered into thinking maybe I'd got it all wrong and there was no girl there. And now he admits there was but there was a perfectly good explanation which sounds perfectly plausible."

"As though Bill Clowes had warned him we might show up," suggested Amy, "and he's had time to get his story together?"

"Right. And that's why I think there was more to it. Because if it was all innocent and okay why not say so in the first place? And even though he'd got a plausible sounding explanation just now, his first response was still denial."

"Exactly. I guess for me personally what I do next depends upon what Nigel the Break-Out Brother goes public with. But I still want to follow it through, even so. I want to know who that girl was and what else went on."

"Me too. Coffee?"

"Please. Americano and a cheese scone."

They took their drinks and snacks to a table in the corner. "So how about trying to locate that children's home?"

"But that name, Cuckoo's Nest, sounds a bit unlikely, don't you think? I mean, I thought that was a jokey name for a madhouse, er, psychiatric hospital."

At least it was a starting point for a search and an obvious next step, though Amy was very conscious of how carefully they would need to tread. A sudden confrontation with the past and whatever had happened back then, if they could trace the girl, could prove very painful for her indeed.

"And we've got to ask, of course, whether we are just needlessly raking up stuff that's best left in the past."

"Yes," Vic agreed. "And the thing for me to focus on is that even though I didn't get her the help she needed because I was prevented from doing that back then, even so by the time she got to the kids' home she would have found all the help she needed. Should have done."

"You can be reassured on that score, certainly," said Amy. "There is another consideration, though. My impression is that Nigel is trying to milk victims' stories for all they are worth simply to make a name for himself. If he manages to track this girl down he could do a lot of damage."

"Okay, so let's just see whether we can confirm Robbo's story for now and see if this Nest place has any record of anyone who could be our girl. Assuming we can actually find it."

"Then we can decide where we go from there."

Vic agreed. "I guess that having to go via this kids' home or refuge or whatever it is, ought to be a kind of safeguard. We need to be ready for some qualified care person to say if we need to back off."

"Okay, let's give it a go." Amy took her tablet from her bag. "Can we get a connection in this place, do you reckon?"

An initial search online turned up nothing at all that looked remotely promising. "But not to worry," said Amy. "We'll track it down somehow even if we have to trawl through all the places within a day's drive.

And that is what they did. First getting a list of all children's homes within five miles of Colinton and then ten miles. "And even if it takes forever," said Amy, "we'll not give up."

It didn't take forever but it did take several days and a lot of patience. "Got it, at last!" Amy called into the phone as soon as Vic picked up. "I've found one. It's Throstle's Nest House and it's the other side of Wigan, towards Skelmersdale. Like Robbo said, it's up the road and round the corner from a supermarket, well a big shopping centre actually. So it looks like it could be the one."

A fortnight after their first cautious contact with Throstle's Nest House, Amy got an email in reply:

> Amy Rashid & Victor Scanlon,
> I am responding to your recent contact with Throstle's Nest House, which has been referred to me. I do not wish to disclose any information here but I think it might be useful for us to meet in person at TNH. Please reply to this email address and hopefully we will be able to make suitable arrangements so that I can have a conversation with you.
> Regards, Wendy Davidson MA, PhD, D Psych.

*

* 5 *

Nigel Clifford

Chapter 13
The Break-out Brother

The time was right, almost right, to think about going public. He would not have to cloak his accusations in vague general terms for much longer. He was gathering actual information about the most serious case. A real, named victim who could help bring down the vile Len Robinson and the despicable Colinton Gilead Hall elders. It had been unbelievably easy to track down the girl in Len Robinson's junk room so it just needed the Bailey girls and Amy the Arab to fill in the details of their own treatment at Robbo's grubby hands. And it should be easy to track those girls down.

There was a minor problem for Nigel in coming out from behind his incognito persona. He needed somehow to tweak that description of himself in order to avoid the possibility of mean-spirited critics and Gilead members finding fault and trying to discredit him. Which was unfortunate really because he was quite proud of his snappy epithet and he didn't want to lose any continuity. He knew that if he simply added his name and called himself "Nigel Clifford, the Break-out Brother and ex-Gilead Elder who found freedom," there would almost certainly be some nit-pickers and hair-splitters who would seize upon the chance to point out that, technically, he never was an elder.

Almost as soon as he had articulated the problem to himself, however, he saw the solution. He would style himself: "The Break-out Brother and ex-Gilead elder who found freedom: Nigel Clifford ably assisted by Alan Clifford." That is, Nigel is the break-out brother and his father is the ex-Gilead elder. But if people choose to read it differently, fine. After all, even though he was not, strictly speaking an elder, once he had broken free and become very active online he had, in effect, become an elder in the online ex-Gilead community. Sorted, problem solved, status retained. And from that point he could move on to thinking about how he would present Jeanette Townley in his forthcoming video about the girl held prisoner in Len Robinson's junk room.

Jeanette was a gem of a find. She really demonstrated the power of social media as a tool for activists and Nigel was going to exploit that power to the full and blow the Fellowship of Gilead apart. A very ordinary Colinton Memories group which his dad liked to dip into on Facebook when he was feeling nostalgic, had first shown him the possibilities. Back when the bulldozers first moved onto Queens Road and began to clear the way for the new flats, someone had put up a post about what a shame it was to think the lovely old houses would be disappearing, and when they asked what memories people had of that supposedly lovely neighbourhood Nigel's first thought was Len Robbo's junk room and the time when he had tried, as a kid, to blow the whistle on his dark secret. So he posted a comment under a pseudonym, Martin Rowland:

> I am sure there are lots of happy memories for lots of you, but for others there are some very troubling ones. I can

> remember a guy who lived along Queens Road who was a high-up in a very strict religious group. But that didn't stop him targetting and abusing vulnerable young kids. And the worst thing about it is that he was never called to account. If there's anyone out there who may have been one of those unfortunate kids, I may be able to help you. Send me a PM if you want to find help or to get your story out there anonymously.

He got lots of replies from obvious time-wasters but one message stood out from the rest:

> Think I know who you mean. He used to come after me and some others in the park. I'd love to track the bastard down. Jeanette.

> Jeanette, thank you for replying. Would you be willing to tell me a little more about your experience with him? I am sure I could help you and anyone else who might be willing to help give him what he deserves. Martin.

After a few messages back and forth she agreed to meet Nigel/Martin near the pagoda at the fountain end of the ornamental lake in the park. Seven o'clock, they said, but by quarter past there was still no sign of her and he was beginning to think that she probably wouldn't show up at all. But then a young woman came into the gardens from beside the old cafe. She was maybe about thirty, tallish and wearing jeans and a black jumper. As Nigel was thinking that this had to be her, she hesitated and walked along the path at the opposite side of the lake. But she kept looking across towards the pagoda as if trying to spot whether the guy waiting beside the lake really was the one she'd arranged to meet and probably trying to pluck up the courage to go ahead with the arrangement. Nigel took a chance and waved to her. She waved back and quickened her pace.

"Jeanette Townley?" he asked as she approached. "I'm, er, Martin Rowland."

"Well, here we are then."

"Yes. Here we are." And what on earth do you say next? How do you begin to ask a total stranger about abuse she suffered as a kid? He suddenly realised he wasn't as well prepared for this as he ought perhaps to have been.

"So you're, what? Sort of gathering evidence against this religious nerd you used to know? Is that it?

"Er, yes. You could put it that way, I guess," he answered. "Do you want to tell me what happened to you?"

"Same as the other girls. And I just thought what you put on Facebook sounded like we might be talking about the same guy. Lived in one of the old houses on Queens Road that they've knocked down, you say?"

"Right."

"Could be the same one. It was over there it always used to happen."

"Like what. Particularly?" Nigel (or Martin Rowland) prompted.

"Usually met him over there where all those trees are. Booze for favours, it was. A half bottle of cheap vodka for a blow job."

"And did he ever take you to his house? Backing on to the park there."

"Oh God, I suppose he might have done. There were others as well. It gets a bit vague."

"Like maybe you got drunk and slept it off at the back of his house?"

"Definitely possible I guess."

"And would he have kept you there? Maybe for quite a long time, I mean."

She didn't really remember any details so he thought he should help her remember. "There was one time I know about when he had a girl in there. Locked in. There was a padlock, you see, which he'd put on the door which looked weird being actually inside the house. So I went round the back one time and looked in from the outside. And there was a girl in there. Could that have been you?"

She smiled broadly. "Hey, right! Do you know which house that was? Who he was? You actually knew the guy?"

"Yes, I knew him, I regret to say."

"Oh wow! That's brill! I'd love to meet him now. Actually come face to face with the bastard and tell him what I think of him. Do you know where he is now?"

He lifted his phone a couple of inches from his shirt pocket and checked that he had the voice recorder running. It would be very useful to have a record of this conversation for future reference when planning his next YouTube videos. A thought suddenly came to him – he could arrange a confrontation, film it secretly. Maybe do it with the Bailey girls as well. A sort of *Len Robinson, This is Your Life*. And what about Amy the Arab? His dad had been able to make contact and already she had agreed to let him visit, so Nigel could tag along and persuade her to co-operate as well. Gosh, what an impact that would have if he could secretly film it, edit it, make sure it was really slick and get it up online! A real knock-out of an impact and they would never recover! It would blow the Gilead Hall right out of the water. But don't rush it, Nigel, he told himself. Don't rush it, this can be very good indeed.

"Look, I don't want to push you into anything," he said to Jeanette, "but maybe just to refresh your memory of what happened, would you come and take a look at something with me?"

"What's that?"

"Well, those big old houses where he lived and where, well... where it happened. There are still a few of them up by the library. Just the same layout as Robinson's old place and they are all empty. So I thought maybe..."

She was looking a bit wary now, as though she might be suspicious and a little worried about what he was up to. He had to tread very carefully. "I just wondered if you could bear to take a look, you know, clarify the details about what he did. If you can. It would help a lot if I could gather as much as possible against this guy because it's really important to bring this guy down. And all the people who brushed everything under the carpet back then."

"You want me to take a look in one of those empty houses? Is that it?"

"That's it. Just take a look, that's all. I promise I won't... I mean, you don't have to. But it would really help if you could."

"Well, okay then."

As they walked slowly from the ornamental gardens towards the playing fields and the park gates beside the Library, he told her of the time when he was a youngster and he had come to investigate

Robbo's junk room secret and had discovered a girl locked in there. "And, gosh, that must have been you."

"Or one of the others."

"Right. So that would be where they all came – to exchange sexual favours for booze, maybe. Or just to sleep off a hangover?"

"Could be both," suggested Jeanette.

"Of course. So anyone sleeping off too much vodka could be there for quite a long time? And maybe kept there just to... Well, you know what I mean."

"Could be, I guess," admitted Jeanette.

"Is that what happened to you, then?"

"Probably. I only really remember that there was this guy at this end of the park who kept me supplied with wine or vodka so he could do as he pleased with me. And I would really love to make that bastard pay for it. Not just for myself, but for the others as well."

"Well I think it will soon be time for him to get his comeuppance. Look, here we are now. Let's try and squeeze through that fence at the end ."

There were three pairs of the old semi-detached houses, empty and derelict, ready for the bulldozer. There was contractor's secure mesh site fencing all around but at the corner two of the sections were not properly fixed together where youngsters had forced them apart so that they could get through and lark around.

Nigel went through first and then helped Jeanette get through and climb across the large heap of rubble piled up in the corner. He led the way to the nearest of the houses which was oriented in the same manner as Robbo's old place. This one had no lean-to at the back, just the single storey extension with a gaping hole in the wall where the window used to be high above the ground. He led the way along the short passage beside the extension and up the few steps to the back door. There was another door at right angles to the main back door and it almost certainly opened directly into the extension. Both doors, however, were secured.

"Let's try and get a look through the window."

They easily found enough stuff to pile up below the window opening and gain the height they needed to look comfortably into the room.

"Right so, over there in the corner is the door we saw just now at the top of the back steps. And right opposite is the doorway into the house itself," Nigel pointed out.

"Yes," Jeanette replied. "I can tell what that stuff is."

"And in the corner over there – the equivalent in Robbo's house – that's where you were. Huddled up looking quite scared. I assume that could have been you?"

"Could've been, I suppose."

"About twenty years ago?"

"I suppose so."

"You would have been quite young then?"

"Young, yes. Bastards they were. All of them. They were bastards. All of those guys."

"There was more than just Robbo?"

"In the park there, yes. Three at least. Bastards they were. And nobody did a fucking thing. Now let's get out of here. I've had enough."

He watched as she disappeared across the far side of the park and then he played back his recording of the conversation. Yes, it was all there, nice and clear. A satisfying evening's work in the cause of anti-Gilead activism. He could describe it that way, of course he could.

There had been one more thing he had wanted to ask: "Would you be willing to confront him?" But he felt that by the end of his time with her she had become rather uneasy and maybe it had got a bit too much for her. Never mind, they'd exchanged phone numbers and email addresses and agreed to meet again to take it further. He could wait to press for setting up a confrontation and maybe try and involve the Bailey girls as well. And even Amy the Arab.

He glanced at his watch. Nine o'clock already. Time to go to the Griffin for a pint of beer or two.

*

Chapter 14
Assembling the Cast

The next step was fairly clear and he needed to get on with it right away. Contacting the Bailey girls shouldn't be too difficult so that was obviously where to begin. It was probably best not to call at the house because David might still be fairly hostile even though Nigel was now long out of all the Gilead rubbish. There were a limited number of schools, though, which the girls might attend so all he needed was a "chance" encounter with one or both of them walking home at the end of the school day which shouldn't be too difficult to set up.

The first school drew a blank. They would both probably look rather different now, being just a few years older, but none of the girls walking past as he watched from his parked car, looked at all recognisable. Nobody on the first day and nobody on the second day either. He was just thinking he might as well drive away and try instead at the other sixth form college later in the week when someone tapped at his window.

It was a man wearing a tweed jacket and a check shirt and carrying a leather briefcase slung over his shoulder.

"Can ask what you are waiting for, sir?" he asked when Nigel wound down the window.

"Er, I was just hoping to catch a friend. Why?"

"I think you should move on now, please."

"What?"

"Will you move on, please, sir."

"I will move on when I am ready," Nigel retorted. The man made no response except to step away a little and just stand by the wall waiting and occasionally peering right into Nigel's car. After a few minutes he moved to the front of the car, mobile phone in his hand, and took a photograph of the number plate before striding away.

Angrily, Nigel drove away as realisation dawned on him. A teacher, it was. A busy-bodying teacher seeing what is not there. Okay, maybe there had been reports of some dodgy-looking person hanging around the school but how on earth can anyone interpret such a perfectly ordinary and innocent thing as waiting to see a friend in such an ugly manner? It was beyond him, that anyone could think in such a way as that teacher evidently had about him, Nigel. Well, all right then. He would leave it until Monday and try again near the other sixth form college.

Irwell Valley College was a little way out of town and further from the Bailey's home – unless they had moved, of course, since Nigel first knew them. It was a fairly busy location, though, with a couple of parades of shops and a small shopping centre so it could get fairly busy at times. And that meant Nigel could more easily merge into the background without looking as if he was lurking and watching the kids as they came out of school.

Lucky first time! As he was strolling past the computer retailer's a small group of girls in school uniform approached from ahead and the girl in the middle with the long brown hair blowing all over the place just had to be Melissa. They got nearer and she was just feet away. "Melissa? Hello there."

She turned towards him, hesitated, and he thought she recognised him. She stopped and gestured to the others. "I'll catch you up." She came across to him.

"Hi, Melissa. It's nice to see you. How are you?"

"I'm good." She looked at the display in the shop window behind him. "What's this? Getting a new computer?"

"Well, looking. Always looking. But, hey, I was hoping I might bump into you or your sister."

She put up her hands in a "go no further" gesture. "No. Stop there. If you're thinking you might drag me back into that Gilead Bible crap, forget it. It's not for me and it never will be, so leave it right there."

He smiled. "I got out of it ages ago. I'm into anti-cult activism now. Building a case against them actually. You might want to take a look at my YouTube channel, 'The Break-out Brother.' There's lots of interesting stuff on there. And the best is yet to come. But, hey, look. Now that we've actually, well, sort of... I mean, it would be great if you'd agree to a chat some time. Get the perspective of a young person being, or resisting, in fact, being dragged in to it."

She looked a little wary but then relaxed. "Okay," she said with a smile. "Invite me for a coffee."

"Great, yes. Fancy a coffee?"

"Sure. Wednesday. That's sports afternoon so I usually manage to get away a bit early. About three o'clock in Enzo's? That's the place down there on the next block."

"Three in Enzo's on Wednesday, then. That's great."

She hurried away to try and catch up with her friends.

All went well on Wednesday, almost too well. Melissa arrived on time and seemed to relish the prospect of being seen in the company of a boyfriend figure who was lots older than the immature lads she knew from school.

"I saw your YouTube stuff," she said when they got their drinks. "Some of it, anyway. Quite slick, I'll give you that, but it's not my thing. All this 'the Bible's just fairy tales' stuff. I mean, sure it is but who cares? Actually trying to prove why it's not true, it's like some nerdy professor trying to tell me why people might think Goldilocks and the three bears is a true story and then proving it isn't. I didn't believe it to begin with so why bother?"

Nigel laughed. "Fair point. But what comes next when I show my face will be rather different. I'm about to go public with all the stuff they sweep under the carpet. It will blow the lid off the Gilead Hall."

"Do tell."

So he told her the story of how he had discovered that Len Robinson kept a very young girl locked in his junk room. "I tried then to do the right thing. But nobody would believe me. Said I was lying – which I wasn't. I'd seen the girl in there and knew for a fact what was going on but all the elders made me keep quiet about it."

"Gosh! And they just let him carry on as if nothing was wrong? And then made me and my sister go round to his house every week for a private Bible study! That's creepy. That's really bad. Yes, you should bring him down. Make him face the facts. Get the police involved, even. He shouldn't be allowed to get away with that."

"He won't be. Not any longer. I'm gathering all the facts together and should be ready fairly soon to go public. Name names instead of hiding behind an alias. I've already traced the girl who was in the junk room. Well, one of them. Looks like there were several others as well. Anyway, this girl's going to help bring him down. I'm going to get her to confront him and get it all on film. But there are just a couple of others as well I need to interview. Not long though and it will all be in the bag."

"Must see that when you go live with it."

"And you will. But look, what I wondered was maybe you'd agree to talk about what it was like for you as a kid having to go to his house for Bible studies and being in there with just you and your sister and creepy Robbo."

She looked a bit shocked at this suggestion and he thought maybe he was expecting a bit too much of her. But she seemed to come round to the idea pretty quickly. "Well, I suppose... Gosh, it's heavy stuff."

"Look, you don't have to commit yourself to it right now. Why don't we just get together in a couple of days and we could start off with a relaxed conversation about things back then."

"Yes fine. Good idea."

"Maybe sometime on Saturday? Would that suit you?"

"Sure. Saturday afternoon."

"Let's meet near the Kenwood Park Library and we can just chat while walking around that area? What about your sister? Jolynne, do you think she might join us?"

"Can't. She's at Uni now. But fine, Saturday afternoon about two o'clock? See you then."

She gathered up her school bag and her sports kit from beside the chair and hurried off home.

As he walked back to his car he thought that what he should do now would be to drop in on his dad on the way home with an update on his case against Robbo and to find out if he'd got any reply yet from Amy the Arab. A face to face with her about whatever it was Robbo was trying with her all those years ago would really help. With that and whatever he might be able to record with Melissa it really would make a great background for the big case against Robbo – and who knows, with Jeanette's help, he might even be able to find more girls who knew the inside of that junk room.

It was all well within his grasp and what was especially nice about it right then was that he could just picture being able to crown a great achievement by taking Melissa for a celebratory meal. And the thought of a date with a very attractive seventeen year old girl was sweet indeed.

It looked as if all was going well with Melissa. She showed up promptly on Saturday afternoon and they took a walk around the park just talking about how things used to be and what a creep Len Robinson was. And to make sure that he had a good record of their conversation to help him with planning the next step, he set his phone's audio recorder running and placed it carefully in his shirt pocket so that it would pick the sound clearly.

"So when you had to go round to his place with your sister for Bible studies, how did you feel about that?" Nigel prompted.

"I hated it, we both did. He was a pervy old creep," she emphasised, "and I really do mean creep. He used to love talking about how we could be bombarded with temptations and how terrible all the people outside of Gilead were. And he would tell us – I was only eleven at the time, Jolynne was thirteen – he would tell us the different ways people would have sex and why they were wrong and why we should always be careful how we dressed. Oh, God, and there was so much more."

"Did he ever… did he ever, er, go too far?"

"Well, if that wasn't going too far… Yes, he did. All the time. I was quite scared of him actually."

Nigel listened, open-mouthed. He began to suspect that Robbo could be far worse even than he had realised. He suggested she should consider talking about it in a little bit more detail, maybe up near where a few of those old houses were still waiting for the bulldozer, and if they could get it on video that would be absolutely brilliant.

"And we could round the whole thing off in due course," he suggested, "with a video sequence of when those houses do eventually fall to the ground. What do you think?"

"Oh, gosh. I'd have to think about that. I'd want to have Jolynne with me."

He realised that he was probably pushing her a little too quickly so he thought it probably best to back off a little for now before trying to record any video with her.

Perhaps if she could have the reassurance of seeing other video sequences of him talking with others who had gone through the Robbo treatment she might more readily agree to taking part in one herself.

So he told her about Jeanette Townley and how she had agreed to go with him all the way to mid Wales to confront him with what he had done to her when he kept her prisoner in his junk room.

"That should be interesting. I don't think I could top that."

This was all going to work out fine with a little caution and patience. It was only a minor problem that Melissa couldn't manage to do more than hint at the really damning stuff against Robbo at this stage, beyond his quite inappropriate talks about sexual behaviour. Which, of course, was all run-of-the-mill stuff in Gilead. It was the way in which the literature always treated the topic and, indeed, the way parents were expected to teach their kids. Nigel himself got just the same gross garbage from his dad when he was very young. Other than the fact the the Bailey girls found Robbo himself very creepy and were bored silly by the Bible study material, it appeared that it would take a little while longer before Melissa would be ready to produce any major bombshells to lob into the middle of Gilead. He was pretty sure, though, that with a little patience he should be able to persuade her to open up about everything he got up to at those Bible study sessions. Like, did he ply them with drink, alcohol for favours like Jeanette had spoken about? Probably even introduced them to some of the other Kenwood Park creeps.

Jeanette, though, was a gem and the video footage he was going to be able to get when he got her to confront Robbo was going to be just mind-blowing. Alongside that some well-edited clips from what Melissa had told him already, it would seal Robbo's fate. All it needed now was to arrange with Jeanette for them to drive down to Porthmadog.

That would have to wait, however, because she was going away for a couple of weeks to Benidorm or somewhere like that. Not to worry, though, it gave him time to go with his dad to the Rashids' home when Amy was going to be there. That turned out to be a useless waste of time, though, because she simply wasn't going to be cooperative. Unbelievably, she was not willing to take the opportunity to expose Gilead for the way they had allowed vulnerable youngsters to be abused. He would simply have to make do with the evidence she had given to the committee which disfellowshipped her. After all, that was a matter of record and she could hardly take it back at this late stage. Willing or not, he would still get her to contribute to the downfall of the Fellowship of Gilead.

The more he thought about Amy's unwillingness to give evidence against Len Robinson and Gilead, the more he became convinced that deep down there was something else going one. And indeed, something which could well become an important topic in his activism to bring Gilead down.

So, Amy the Arab was clearly a victim of Robinson's abusive behaviour. But now she was actually being quite defensive of him, and of Gilead as well. This looked very much like a clear case of Stockholm Syndrome which is shown in victims of often very severe abuse developing a strong attachment to their abusers. It was so patently obvious: Amy the Arab had suffered far more at the hands of Len Robinson than just the inappropriate touching she had once been quite open about.

This could be big. Very big indeed. And widespread. And now he, Nigel Clifford, the Break-out Brother, was going to make a name for himself as the one who would put an end to the Fellowship of Gilead once and for all.

*

* 6 *

Len Robinson

Chapter 15
True and Timely Repentance

Len Robinson was well aware of his tendency to fall prey to sin but, being aware of his weakness he was able to keep it under control. As an elder in the congregation, it often fell to him to give counsel to others who had succumbed to their own sinful tendencies and to help adjust their thinking and enable true repentance. It would perhaps come as a surprise to ordinary members of the congregation if they were to realise the prevalence even among faithful Christians of struggles to keep the misuse of sexuality under control.

Len's keen awareness of the frequent sinfulness of others served a good and wholesome purpose: it reminded him constantly of God's forgiving nature in response to true repentance; it gave him confidence that he would be able, when at last the end came in sight, to make true and timely repentance for his own very minor misdeeds. And, of course, it showed how utterly depraved the world outside the Christian congregation must be without belief in God or the loving and wise direction from his organisation on earth.

He was confident, therefore, when the little hussy from the fairground came prowling around, that he would not allow her to push his perfectly understandable weakness to breaking point. And, indeed, she did not. He resisted almost every temptation, and at first it was very easy to do so. The occasions when she did tempt him beyond his power to resist were so very few that true and timely repentance would be no problem.

He caught her late on a June Sunday afternoon, the final day of the annual funfair on Kenwood Fields. He had spent the day in Christian service, going from door-to-door seeking out meek sheeplike people (there were very few) who might be willing to listen and respond to the good news of the Kingdom of God. And then he had driven to neighbouring Radleigh where he was the visiting speaker. He returned home at tea-time, fired up with zeal for the truth of God and as he walked in through his front door, he caught sight of someone hurrying to escape from the house by the open kitchen window. He gave chase and caught the intruder before she could get herself through the window.

She was probably about ten years old with untidy long brown hair. She was wearing shabby blue jeans and a grey tee-shirt and although she was scruffy and obviously frightened, she was really quite an attractive kid.

"Who are you?" he demanded.

She didn't reply.

"Where are you from?"

She pointed towards the fields.

"From the fairground?"

She said nothing.

"How many houses have you been into?"

She said nothing.

"How many?" he demanded again.

"No! No, no, no!"

"Only my house?"

She kept quiet.

"Have you taken anything?"

She shook her head.

She didn't appear to have anything at all. He took her back into the house. "Show me where you were. Did you go upstairs?"

She shook her head.

"Which rooms did you go in?"

She pointed to the front room, the one he used as the meeting room.

"Show me where you went."

She hesitated and then let him take her into the room.

Nothing seemed to have been disturbed. "Where else did you go?"

She shook her head.

"Nowhere else? What about the back room over there, did you go in there?"

"No! No!"

Again she let him take her into the room. He stood in front of his desk and checked that nothing appeared to have been disturbed. He pointed to the drawers. "Did you look in those drawers?"

"No."

"Did you open that cupboard?"

"No."

"Very well. Now listen to me. If I ever catch you or any of your friends in here ever again I will take you straight to the police. Do you understand?"

She nodded.

He led her to the back door. "Go on, now. Away you go."

She didn't run. She walked slowly to the bottom of the garden, constantly looking back as he watched her. Then she climbed over the fence at the gap in the hedge and he came inside, bolting the door behind himself.

When he looked out on Monday morning the fairground lorries and trailers and caravans were already moving away. He went downstairs, made himself some breakfast and about an hour later went to his shed to gather together all the tools he needed for the day's work. He went into the lean-to for some sacks of compost. And the girl was back there, huddled in the corner looking very frightened.

He was about to start shouting at her and send her away once more but he stopped himself. He hurried down to the bottom of the garden and looked out over the fence. The last of the fairground trucks were slowly forming into a convoy to drive out of the park at the Library gateway. Before he could get back to the house they would all be on their way. Gone. Off to their next location, nearby or far away. And the scruffy girl was still in his lean-to.

"They're going," he said to her when he returned. "All of them. What are you going to do now?"

She huddled herself tighter into the corner, almost as if she was expecting a thrashing. There was no real damage she could do out there in the lean-to so he turned his back on her and went into the house. Then, after a second mug of tea he double-checked that all the windows were secure and drove off to work for the day.

She was still there when he came home at the end of the afternoon, Still huddled in the corner looking frightened and looking like she hadn't moved all day. "Hey! It's time you cleared off!" he snapped at her.

He walked closer to her and she cried out, “No! No, please! Don’t hit me!”

“You need to go away.”

“No! Don’t make me go away.”

Don’t make her go away? In fact he wasn’t too surprised at that because now the fairground had packed up and left it probably meant there was nowhere she could go.

“You came with the fairground, didn’t you? That’s where you belong, isn’t it?”

“Yes. No.”

“Yes, no? What do you mean by that? Yes, no. Stupid girl. I can take you back to them, you know. Do you want that? Shall I take you? Where are they now, do you know?”

“No, no, don’t take me away! Please don’t take me away!”

The thought had crossed his mind whilst he had been working and really the solution was quite easy. At least for a short time. All it needed was for him to open up the blocked off doorway from the top of the back door steps into the utility room so that if necessary she need not be out in the cold all night. He already had a spare padlock so he could make sure that she would not be able to get from the utility room into the house. There was a tap and an earthenware sink in there and she could have a towel and a bucket. He would bring down his old camp bed and get her a blanket and she would have everything she needed. And she could have a sandwich now and again. That would give him time to work out what he could do next, if need be.

It would have been fine if it had only been for a couple of days. But it dragged on and she showed no inclination to leave. After a few days it became all too obvious that she needed more than a tap, a towel and a bucket. She needed to be able to have a bath – but he was not going to allow her to take the opportunity to sneak around anywhere in the house. So it was only reasonable that he should supervise her bathing. She was reluctant to take her clothes off. Understandably, no doubt, but she had to do it. She became quite stubborn, though, and wanted to keep her knickers on.

"Don't be stupid," he said. "You can't keep them on in the bath." And as he pulled them down and made her step out of them something fell to the floor. It was his driving licence and two credit cards which he must have left on his desk without realising that he had not put them back in his wallet. His passport was there as well which meant she had been rooting about in his desk drawers, and there was a necklace she must have found in someone else's house.

"Where did you get these?" he demanded.

"I was… I… was… I was going to... don't know."

"So you did go into my study, didn't you? You looked though the drawers, didn't you? What else did you take?

"Nothing."

"What else?

"Nothing! Nothing! I didn't take anything from your drawer."

"Of course you did, you stupid girl! How else could you have got my cards? And this necklace. You've been in other people's houses as well. Haven't you? We'll have to give this back. Now get into the bath."

She stepped into the bath and he sat on the stool and looked on as she washed herself, but she didn't do it very thoroughly so he had to help her. He smiled at her as he soaped away the grime of her recent misadventures. "You're really a very pretty little girl, you know. Yes, very pretty..."

When she was finished and dried he took her downstairs wrapped in a large towel and let her sit with him in the front room while her clothes were washed and tumble dried. And late in the evening he took her back to the utility room and padlocked the door.

She could have walked away at any time but she did not. She let him help her in the bath a second time and a third time and he thought maybe she actually enjoyed it. He never did anything inappropriate beyond washing her, except once but he did say he was sorry and promised not do do it again. And for the most part he kept that promise. And still she did not walk away.

*

Chapter 16
Moving On

All would have been well had it not been for the retarded young Scanlon boy. He came calling at the house for no apparent reason and then had the nerve to go snooping round the back and peering through windows. And, of course, when he saw the girl he thought the worst. People like that always do think the worst of people in positions of authority and leadership. They never stop to think that there may be a perfectly good reason for things and that those who take the lead are doing their very best for everybody. Oh no, young Scanlon would never stop to think of that. And off he goes, tittle-tattling to Bill Clowes.

Well, he ought to have realised that Bill would not be taken in by his stupid tales and it showed what a nasty little piece of work young Scanlon was. Of course, once the suspicion had been raised, no matter how far-fetched it was, Bill was obliged to follow it through, but discreetly of course. So he called round a few days later to lay the whole silly tale to rest.

"... to lay it to rest. Yes, of course. Yes, do come in," said Len as he led his senior colleague into the front room, and carefully avoiding direct sight of the padlocked door.

"No need to be alarmed," Clowes reassured him as he settled his bulk into a rather too small chair. "But, as you know, with the Regional Overseer's visit in a couple of weeks we need to be sure that we have covered every possibility."

"Every possibility?" queried Len apprehensively.

"What I'm thinking, you see, is that in case – and it is only in case, if you get my drift. But what if Scanlon senior were to somehow let it slip to the RO?"

"Oh, I don't think he would do that. He is very firm, you know, with the boy. Very firm, won't stand for any nonsense from him."

"Yes, I know that. But I mean suppose he were to ask for advice on handling such a difficult youngster? Like, I mean, suppose he says something like, 'You'll never believe the tales he tells.' And then he gives a for instance and says, 'How do I stop him saying things like that?' And so, before you know it the sordid little tale is on its way around and sooner or later someone somewhere is going to wonder. So we need to, how shall I put it? We need to pre-empt that. You get my drift?"

"Yes, I see what you mean."

"So we need to make absolutely double sure there's not an ounce of truth in it. So you tell me now that is the case."

"Well of course it is. Not an ounce."

"Very good. So what next?"

"Next? How do you mean?"

"Suppose for a minute if this did get out, is there anyone who might wonder if it could be true?"

"I wouldn't think so. Surely not."

"Well most wouldn't but some might. I mean young Scanlon believed it, after all."

"Yes but he's a retarded little twerp."

"Ah but others could be, you know, taken in. Like what about – and I'm not saying that they would – but what about maybe Omar and Linda Rashid? They're right on the edge, you know. Not as spiritually strong as they ought to be. And very protective of young Amy. You have to think about it, you know."

This was getting very uncomfortable. Was Bill Clowes hinting at anything? Had anyone said anything? Complained? Surely not. He had never overstepped the mark with Amy. An arm round her waist, drawing her close maybe, and a hand on her bottom but only ever over her skirt and never anything inappropriate. He shifted uneasily in his seat and didn't know how to respond to what Clowes was saying.

"You know what I think?" Clowes continued. "A very good idea for you to think about, and Freda suggested this one as well..."

Freda? Did he mean he had been talking about it with his wife? Of course he would have done. Elders always told their wives all about the salacious tales from confidential "shepherding" visits with straying members. That was one of the things that helped to keep the rumour mill going.

"What we suggest is that you could organise a gathering. You know, one Saturday have an open house evening. We could sing Gilead songs, have Bible quizzes, cakes and soft drinks. And leave everywhere open so people can wander about as they please. You know, sandwiches in one room, cakes in another, drinks somewhere else. And then if this silly tale ever gets out, people will think, no that can't be right. We've been in Brother Robinson's house and he doesn't have anything at all to hide. There, now. What do you think of that?"

What Len thought was that Bill Clowes suspected there might be some truth in the tale and that it was time for him put things right. "Yes, that's worth thinking about. I'll, er, see what I can do."

He ushered Clowes out of the house, taking care to keep him away from the padlocked door. The padlock was his big mistake. Without it young Scanlon would perhaps not have been tempted to come snooping around to see what might be behind the door. Maybe he should have put up a curtain. A long curtain across the door to keep out the draughts and conceal the padlock from view. That was a lesson to be learned. Not of course that there would ever be another occasion. But we all have our little weaknesses and we ought not to allow them to go on public view. It was all in the past now – almost – and he could easily ensure that nothing else could find its way into the rumour mill.

It was getting ever nearer to the point for a timely and true repentance, except that the girl was still in the utility room and he was not yet sure how she was to be removed. First, though, another bath time. He unlocked the door and brought her out. "Upstairs," he said. "Come along. Into the bathroom."

It would probably have to be the final time but it did not prevent him from appreciating her young beauty as she undressed and stepped into the bath. He watched her and washed her and avoided doing anything inappropriate even though it would probably be the last opportunity. Later that night, as he lay awake wondering how he was to remove her, he could not help thinking how good it would feel if he could take it to the next level with her. But, no. No, he must stop himself even thinking it.

How was he to remove her though? A couple of weeks before, when first she had arrived and had seemed determined not to leave, he had guessed she was trying to run away from a bad situation with the fairground people. But only now did he recall when he first caught her he had threatened her with the police if she were to come back. And now he realised that was probably what she actually wanted. Why else would she have dared to return? If he had taken her to the police they would have helped her to escape from harm. Was that it? And she needed help to find them in a strange town she did not know.

Right at the beginning he could have done it. Not now, though. Not after the bath times and the very few indiscretions. He could not risk having her tell the police about any of that. What was he to do? Dawn was breaking and still he had not slept. He had to find a plan. He would not be able to relax until he knew exactly what he could do to clear the way for his timely and true repentance.

What if she were to… ? He could take her in his van, hitch up a small digger from Darley Plant Hire and leave her deep somewhere she would never be found. No. No, no, no, no. No, not at all, never. How could he let such a thought even come into his head? No, no, no. He woke a little later and it was still there tormenting him as if he had actually done it and the police knew and they were coming for him and it wasn't until his alarm sounded and his radio switched on, that he woke properly to the reality. It was a vile thought planted in his mind by the devil.

It was the devil and his demons who had brought the girl to him in the first place. It was clear now. They knew his weakness, they knew how a pretty girl could tempt him, and they had exploited his secret dreams of pleasure. But no more. He would find a solution and he would not rest until he had done so.

The solution would have to be like this: he would be kind; he would be helpful; he would do no harm. There would be no repercussions, not now and not in the future. It would be as if nothing had ever happened. Except that the girl – he still did not know her name – would look back a long time hence and, if she should remember him, she would remember him as the one who helped her. And the solution to accomplish all that would be found that day.

After a day of judicious asking around and picking up leaflets from the local authority housing department, the Citizens' Advice Bureau and the Children in Need charity shop, he had the bare bones of a plan. He would need to drive right out of the area, somewhere completely unconnected with Colinton. And there, wherever that drive took him, he would need to find a children's care home or whatever they are called. And they would take her in and she would be looked after and all would be well.

It took two days of lost work and nearly a couple of hundred miles driving but he found the right sort of place – Throstle's Nest House, which was a good distance beyond Manchester and completely unconnected with Colinton. One more day of not working and earning but first a final bath time to enjoy and then the problem would be solved.

He took her the following day, left her with clear instructions about going into the building and then drove away, round the corner and onto the supermarket car park. And from the payphone in the supermarket foyer, he phoned Throstle's Nest House and told them to look out for a homeless girl who had come in. He reached into his pocket and took hold of that necklace he could no longer hand over to anyone without the risk of linking back to himself and his very minor indiscretions. He dropped it into a waste bin by the supermarket entrance. After all it was probably fake and of hardly any value. Then he drove home.

It was a tremendous relief to have resolved the situation, of course it was. To be able to feel that nobody was likely to stumble across anything which might lead to any misunderstanding, or arouse totally unwarranted suspicions. But it was nice while it lasted, having that lovely little girl in the house. Buying a change of clothes for her from the charity shop and new knickers from Dobymart. And it was nice to have been able to keep a pair of her old... Well, it was nice.

But now was the time to leave all that behind, to focus upon his role as an elder in leading the congregation in the service of God Our Father and being well prepared for the Regional Overseer's visit. The distractions and temptations were all in the past now and the only interaction he ever had with young girls was all, or mostly at any rate, in the Gilead Hall where it was plainly obvious to everyone that there was nothing whatever to give cause for concern or to tittle-tattle about.

There were a few pretty young girls in the congregation so Len was able to exercise his talent for relating to young ones to good and beneficial effect. The Rashid girl, though, started to distance herself and when she was around thirteen or so she took to wearing a head scarf Arab style which was hardly a good thing. He tried to point out to her that she was falling in line with what was, after all, a Muslim pagan practice which was not at all appropriate for a young woman of Gilead. But she took no notice. He would have taken the matter up with her father but none of the other elders thought it was a problem so he let it slide.

After that everything bumbled along very nicely and it was very clear that the congregation continued to have the blessing of God Our Father. Especially after they disfellowshipped that brainless little twerp Vic Scanlon and then, a few years later, the Rashid girl. Both for really quite brazen gross misconduct. And then, of course, Alan Clifford took himself off in a tantrum. No loss there, however, because he always was a bit of a wimp. All in all everything was fine and all the more so when Len's uncle who was never a man of Gilead died and left him his house in a lovely secluded valley in Merionethshire.

Ages after he had settled in at his new home he got a message from Bill Clowes.

> Dear Len, I thought you should know that the Rashid girl and Vic Scanlon have been snooping around looking for you. Muck raking, I suspect so in case they turn up on your doorstep, forewarned is forearmed as they say. Regards, Bill Clowes.

All that nonsense which young Scanlon had concocted out of nothing was long in the past, so it would be very easy to be prepared for him if he were to show up once again snooping around for excuses to make trouble. Len needed to make sure that if he did show up when there was nobody around he would not be able to find anything in the yard or the shed or the old stable block that he could turn into something embarrassing. Inside the house itself was no problem, of course, because even though he rarely had visitors and he was always careful to tidy up.

So let them come. He would even extend to them a friendly welcome because, after all, as an elder even though he did not have any specific responsibilities in his new congregation, he was allowed some exceptions to the requirement to break off all connection with disfellowshipped persons, so he could take the opportunity to show them beyond all doubt how foolish they were to slander the Fellowship of Gilead. Let them come.

*

* 7 *

Lisa

Chapter 17
Lisa's Story

Most people know where they come from, who their mum and dad were, where they went to school and things like that, but Lisa was different. She had a big sister who was stupid and there was a woman who said she was their mum but she wasn't nice and she never did mum type things and then she got taken away because she had done something bad to one of her customers. She told Lisa and her sister to run away before that happened and before they could be taken away as well. She said she would come for them when the police let her go but she never did and then Lisa had to escape again because the place her sister took her wasn't nice so she climbed onto the back of a lorry and went away and her sister wasn't there any more. And that was all she knew for sure but she wasn't going to think about it or talk about or tell anyone else at all because it was horrible. Maybe one day she would but not yet because she never ever wanted to go back to any of those places or those people ever again.

She had other memories after all that stuff but they were jumbled up like pictures in a box that didn't belong together. They weren't like one, two, three, four, five, when you know what comes first and what comes next. They were more like seven, twenty-four, twelve, four, nineteen but they wouldn't go into order and lots of them were missing or they were hidden in the shadows of dark places. The earliest pictures she had that she didn't just want to forget about, that had numbers on them and went into a proper order were from long after she had escaped on the lorry. There were some others who helped her to go stealing but she ran away from that as well and hid somewhere.

Then she came to Throstle's Nest House. She had been in the back of a van for hours and hours or maybe only a few minutes when it stopped and the man came round to the back and opened the doors and after all the darkness and gloom of the ride the light was too bright for her eyes.

"All right, you can get out now," he said. "Go to that seat over there. See it? Underneath the big tree?"

She blinked and rubbed her eyes and looked around. Up and down and along the busy road. It was very confusing and noisy and windy. But she could see a long wooden bench underneath a huge tree with bare branches.

"Go and sit there and stay there until you have seen my van disappear. Do you understand?"

She nodded.

"Do you understand? He repeated.

She nodded again but she was starting to panic. Was he going to go away? Go away and leave her on her own? She didn't like him, he was horrible and nasty like a lot of the others that she didn't want to think about and now he was going to go away and leave her on her own and that was frightening.

"Do you understand?" he repeated once more.

No, no, no, she didn't understand. "What's going to happen to me?" She began to sob. This was horrible, a different sort of horrible and she didn't know what she was going to do.

“When you see my van disappear round the corner you must walk along that lane up to the big house. Do you see it there at the other side of the grass? The big house there with the red door?”

She nodded.

“Go inside and wait. And somebody will come and take care of you. Do you understand?”

She nodded.

“As soon as I get round the corner I will phone and tell them you have arrived. Do you understand?” he repeated.

She nodded again. Understand, stand stand stand under under under understand.

“Go on, then. Off you go.”

She walked slowly toward the big tree where the seat was and when she looked back the van was driving away along the busy road. It stopped at some traffic lights. She carried on to the seat which was covered with bird shit. And she stood under, under the tree and sat under the tree. Understand and sit. When she looked back along the road the van was driving away again. It turned a corner and disappeared from sight. She waited a few moments and then stood up and thought that maybe she should run away as far as she could but instead she walked towards the big house like the man told her to do. Throstle’s Nest House, it was, but she didn’t know that was what it said on the big board at the side of the door.

It was bigger on the inside than the outside. The big front door was as tall as a tree and she stepped inside a room with a ceiling as high up as a roof and stairs that were wide enough for cars and buses and went high enough to reach the chimneys. She hesitated for a little while and looked around. To one side of the stairs there was a big wide table where a lady was talking with another lady and a young boy. At the other side of the stairs a lady in a white coat was watering plants on the window sill. She came across when she saw Lisa.

"Hello. Have you come to see someone?"

Lisa shook her head.

"Oh. Waiting for someone?"

"Yes."

"Who? Is there someone I can go and get for you?"

"Don't know."

"Come through here and and sit down," said the lady and she guided her into a room where there were lots of seats and some little tables. "Would you like a drink? A glass of orange juice?"

Lisa nodded.

The lady came back a few minutes later with a glass of juice and some biscuits and she sat down with Lisa. After a while the lady said, "Are you going to tell me your name?"

"Lisa."

"I'm Wendy. And where are you from, Lisa?"

"The van. He brought me in the van."

"Who brought you?"

"The man."

"He brought you in the van?"

Lisa nodded.

"And where do you live?"

"Near his house. No, anywhere. Don't know."

"And what is his name? Do you know?"

Lisa shrugged her shoulders.

"Do you not know his name? The man who brought you here."

She shook her head.

"So is he your dad?"

Lisa shook her head.

"Do you know why he brought you here?"

"Didn't want me in his shed."

"Where are your mum and your dad?"

Lisa shrugged her shoulders and then she began to cry. Wendy put her arms around her and hugged her until she felt calm again and she drank some more juice.

Then Wendy said, "Are you waiting for somebody to come and collect you to take you home?"

"No!" said Lisa. "No, no, no!" And she began to cry again.

Then the other lady who had been talking with the boy and his mum came into the room and whispered something to Wendy. They went over to the far side where Lisa couldn't hear what they were saying and after a few minutes Wendy came back.

"We had a telephone call just now," she said. "He didn't say who he was but he told us you need to be somewhere safe. Is that right?"

"Safe, yes."

"Well you are certainly safe with us."

Wendy was nice and she promised that she wasn't going to make her go back to wherever she had come from. She even got some other nice people to come and help and they found a room with a bed and some other things and they said she could stay until they knew where she belonged and they didn't mean the place where she had come from, they meant the place where she really belonged and people loved her. And Lisa said she didn't think she deserved to have nice things and nice people because she was a dirty little slut.

There were other people they wanted her to talk to and that was okay because they promised they were not going to make her go anywhere she didn't want to or didn't feel safe. There was Frank who was another of the doctors like Wendy except that he only came two or three times a week and didn't live at Throstle's Nest like Wendy. But first there were Geoffrey and Marian who were police and that was a bit scary because maybe they thought she had been doing some naughty things but she didn't really know. They did say that they wouldn't take her away and that they only wanted to find out what had happened to her so they could stop it happening again to her or anyone else. So that was probably okay and, after all, Lisa did know better than to tell the police anything at all that she didn't want them to know.

So when they came she said, "No," or "Don't know," to everything and then Wendy said they should leave her alone so eventually they did.

It was like coming along a narrow passageway, getting to Throstle's Nest House in the white van. A passageway with high walls and locked doors and windows in the shadows. But she wasn't shut in anywhere, she wasn't the wrong side of a locked door. It was different behind those doors, where she couldn't go. She couldn't remember properly what was on the other side or in the shadows, only that she was glad she wasn't there any longer. Some people said maybe she should try being hypnotised because it might help her get to the other side of those doors and windows and remember what had happened to her before she came to Throstle, who she was, where she had come from. But, no, she definitely didn't want to go there because she thought it was too frightening so they didn't make her do it. One day, maybe. One day she would be able to do it, but not yet.

Sometimes it was as if she could nearly see it if she wanted to. It was bright enough for her to see everything far away at the end of the passage, where she had started and could remember but didn't want to talk about, even to herself. But the bright light hurt her eyes and when she tried to see the doors and windows and the things in the shadows, where she had been before she came to Throstle, she couldn't see anything. Sometimes it felt as though she was one of the shadows and she had strayed away from the real Lisa.

When she had been there a few days and still hadn't seen the things in the passageway, they said they would help her get a birth certificate which would make everything easier for her to be part of the great big Throstle's Nest family and then eventually get a job and have a flat in the hostel. But it meant she had to tell them who her mum was and where she was from. And they found out that someone back then with the same name as her mum had been sent to prison for some really bad stuff and the police were looking for her daughter who was fifteen and was missing.

Then Wendy asked her – very kindly and with a smile – was she maybe a lot older than she looked?

"No," said Lisa. "No. Can't be. My sister was older but I was only ten, I think, when we ran away. Eleven now."

"Your sister? You have a sister? You never told us about her."

"I didn't want to. Never wanted to go back there." She began to cry and Wendy came to her and put her arms around her and they sat together on the long bench by the window.

"So what was your sister's name?" Wendy asked.

"Hazel."

After a few minutes of just comforting her in silence, Wendy asked "Was there maybe another time after your mum had been arrested when just your sister was missing but you were not? Were you maybe with someone else? A grandparent, perhaps?"

"No. Couldn't be. I never went back. Don't know about Hazel."

It was easy to tell that Wendy was thinking hard about something, trying to figure something out. She had the sort of eyes that seemed to say, don't stop me, I'm thinking. And then she said, "I think maybe I know why Central Registry couldn't find a birth record for you. Do you think perhaps your mum might never have registered your birth?"

Lisa just nodded very sadly and more tears started to come into her eyes and she could feel them running down her face. She looked up at Wendy. "Would that be why... why, she never let me go to school like Hazel?"

"Could be," Wendy replied softly.

And then Lisa remembered something horrible. Once she got very poorly, feeling very achy and hot and coughing all the time and her mum wouldn't let her go to the doctor but took Hazel and made her pretend to be poorly so they could get some medicine and Lisa could have it. Only the doctor thought Hazel was faking it to get some time off school and she couldn't get the right medicine that Lisa needed. "That's what my mum was like."

Wendy didn't say anything. She just put her arms around her and hugged her again while she had a cry, and Lisa thought Wendy was having a cry as well. And then after a few minutes she said, "Look, you don't have to worry about anything at all now. We know your birthday and where you were born. And we know where you mother is, of course. So we have everything we need to make sure that we get everything done that needs to be done. You're safe now, Lisa."

She went back up to her little room and actually began to feel happy. Happy to be at Throstle's Nest House and she just wanted to say, thank you, thank you, thank you to Wendy for just being Wendy. And the silly thing, well not completely stupid silly, was that she wanted to say thank you to the nameless man who brought her here. Except that if she ever did he would probably pull her knickers down and spoil it.

*

* 8 *

Nigel Clifford

Chapter 18
Confrontation

Jeanette spent the night at Nigel's flat so that they would be able to get off to an early start for the long drive to Mid Wales in the morning. She was so much lovelier than any of the girls from the Griffin, and lovelier too than any of the girls he had ever known during all his years in Gilead. She woke earlier than him and was already finding things in the kitchen to make breakfast. Could anything have felt better than this?

"When this thing with Robbo is done," he suggested later as he cleared away the breakfast things, "it would be good if we could get together and… Well, I think we get along pretty well, you and me."

She smiled but said nothing.

Three hours later they were driving out of Porthmadog and approaching Cwm Croeswen. "How do you feel about this? Still okay? No misgivings?"

"Never felt better,"Jeanette replied. "That bastard's going to have to pay now for everything he did to me and to those others years ago."

Nigel slowed the car as he looked for the turning into the cwm. The driver behind would just have to be patient. At last they found it and drove carefully along the poorly surfaced lane to Ty Croeswen at the end.

"Oh my God," said Jeanette. "What a creepy weird place this is! Just right, I suppose, for that pervy old git."

Before getting out of the car Nigel got his action camera, a small video camera that could be dashboard mounted, bike helmet mounted or just discreetly hand held to give good quality video. He wasn't going to take any chances here, he would get the whole thing recorded. Jeanette was checking something in her shoulder bag.

"Okay," she said. "I'm good to go."

They scrunched across the gravel and knocked loudly at the front door. No response.

"Oh for fuck's sake!" said Jeanette. "Don't say we've come all this way for nothing."

Nigel knocked again. They heard sounds from within and at last the door opened.

"Hello, Len. Remember me? Yes, of course you remember me."

"Oh yes. Nigel, isn't it? Er, hello."

"Are you going to invite us in?"

"Well, no. No, I shouldn't. You were disfellowshipped. I can't talk with you."

"Yes, you can. And I really do think you will want to hear what we have to say. Do you know who this is?" he added, gesturing towards Jeanette.

"No. No, who are you?"

"She is the girl who you kept in your junk room years ago. Remember?"

"Oh right," he said, apparently not too alarmed. "Yes, the others were asking about you. A few weeks ago. Yes, I took you to Throstle's Nest House – there I remember it now. So how are you?"

"Are you going to invite us in, then?" Jeanette asked.

"Yes, of course. Do come inside."

"What's this Throstle's Nest House?" Nigel whispered as they followed him into the house.

"No idea. Must be one of the others."

"So then," said Jeanette when they came into his gloomy living room. "Half bottle of vodka for a blow job again, shall we?"

"What? What are you talking about?"

"Oh. Do you not do that any more. Pity. Never mind. I've got something for you though."

She reached into her bag and produced a knife. An ordinary eight inch meat carver. And she plunged it hard into him just below the rib cage. "That's from all of us. From all the girls you and your pervy friends did your stuff with. Bye bye. See you in hell."

"Right," she said, turning to Nigel. "Let's get out of here."

He followed her. Obediently, gobsmacked and speechless, he followed her and drove. Just drove. In whatever direction, it didn't matter. Any direction. He just drove. And he said nothing.

"Pull over," she said after twenty minutes or so. "Up ahead. There's parking up ahead. Pull in there."

There was a large lorry in the lay-by. "No, carry on. Try the next one," she said.

After a few more miles they came to an empty lay-by where they could pull in and park out of sight of the road. As soon as they had stopped, Jeanette wriggled out of her jumper and her jeans, bundled them into a plastic bag and took things from her bag. Then, satisfied that she had no blood showing anywhere on her, she took the plastic bag and stuffed it into the waste bin beside the lay-by.

As they drove away and gathered speed she began to laugh. An easy, now-we-can-relax sort of laugh. "Oh wow!" she said. "That feels so good! It was so much better than I could have imagined. Do you realise we did it and there is no way anyone can ever trace it back to us? Thank you so much! You've been a star!"

She was quite possibly right about it not being traceable back to them. There would be no CCTV footage in the vicinity of Cwm Croeswen; there was nobody around to have seen the car at Robbo's house; his action camera was in his pocket and he could easily dispose of the memory card. He hadn't told anyone, not even his dad, that he was planning to visit Robbo that day. And, to cap it all, it could well take a long time before anybody would discover that there was anything amiss in that dismal cottage in the middle of nowhere. He knew that he really ought to report the matter right away to the police, but this gave him time to take stock, to think things through, and to be very clear in his mind what he was going to do next.

Jeanette didn't want to go straight home when they got back to Colinton which was entirely understandable. Nor did she want to eat anything and neither did Nigel, so they went straight to bed. And as he reached out to put an arm around her, he remembered the car behind them on the main road. That driver had seen them. Seen them looking for Cwm Croeswen. Whoever it was had had lots of time to take note of their car. Maybe had a dashcam running. Could probably give a good description of their car.

No, he could not assume he had time to take stock and work out carefully what his next move should be. Too late to cover his tracks. Too late to go straight to the police. He was completely and utterly caught up in a crime he had not planned and it was too late now for him not to be guilty. Accessory to murder. All he could do was hope that it would take a long time before the awful scene inside Ty Croeswen was discovered.

He was in shock. That's what it was; he had responded in shock to what had happened. He wasn't thinking straight, he just followed the natural instinct to run. So, yes, he did still have a chance to do the right thing. No more delay. Just get down to the police station right away and tell them everything that had happened.

He lay awake all night seeing it again and again as Jeanette thrust that knife in. A single thrust deep into exactly the right place. Her change of clothes. And her laughter and exhilaration when she had binned the blood-stained jeans and jumper. She had known exactly what she was going to do. She had used him to find her victim.

Only now did he realise that she was probably not the girl he had seen in Robbo's junk room all those years ago. It had been too easy to find her. He should have suspected it. Robbo was simply a convenient scapegoat, a proxy to take the place of all the other shadowy figures against whom she had harboured a perfectly understandable murderous grudge.

He glanced at his watch. Seven thirty. He should get up, get dressed and take Jeanette home. And then get down the police station while there was still time to avoid the guilt of an accessory.

Jeanette reached out to him. “Don’t go. Stay with me a bit longer.”

They stayed in bed another hour before Nigel got dressed but Jeanette showed no sign at all of wanting to move. Nigel pottered around the flat doing bits and pieces of not much at all and then doing it all again as he waited for Jeanette to get up. When at last she came into the living room it was nearly midday. All she wanted was a piece of toast and a mug of coffee and to sit staring at the floor.

“Shall I take you home now?” Nigel suggested.

“No. Not yet. Let me stay here. Please.”

So she stayed. And stayed, and time went on and with it, Nigel’s chances of successfully pleading not guilty to a charge of accessory to murder diminished further and further. The day dragged on and it was bedtime again. Nigel knew that he should slip out and… but he didn’t. He went to bed with Jeanette.

In the morning, with the prospect of spending all of Monday in just the same way they had spent Sunday, Nigel dressed. He made coffee. And then at last he slipped out leaving Jeanette still in his bed. He walked into the town centre and stopped near to the steps in front of the police station. He looked up at the glass doors and carried on walking in the direction of the town hall.

He looked back. And the big dominant thought in his mind was that in the hours since that awful deed he’d had sex with Jeanette four times. He went straight home. Right or wrong, he would not betray her. He would stand alongside her and let her decide when they should give themselves up.

When he got home Jeanette had gone. It was important, of course, to get back into a normal routine as far as possible so he sent her a message via Facebook suggesting that they should get together for a chat fairly soon. And then he set about getting ready to do a day's work and and try to focus upon the way forward.

As he neared home at the end of the afternoon he couldn't stop seeing, in his imagination, several police cars waiting on the spare ground at the rear of his flat with blue lights still flashing. And as he drove towards his ramshackle lock-up garage all the police officers would emerge from their vehicles and approach him menacingly. But there was nobody there except a couple of boys kicking a ball around.

He locked his car and his ladders away and went up to his flat. He checked his phone and his laptop. No emails, no message from Jeanette. Tuesday was exactly the same, and so was Wednesday and he began to allow himself to feel a little relieved that he had not immediately had that dreaded visit from the police.

He kept a regular eye on the BBC online news pages, checking for reports local to Porthmadog. Nothing. Just various road accidents, a mountain rescue up in Snowdonia, weather reports. Nothing. And still nothing by the end of the week or into the next. The longer it took for the gruesome discovery to be made, the greater the chance that whoever was driving behind while they were looking for Cwm Croeswen would never make any connection with the car in front driving a little slower than normal.

All might just be well. But there was still no message from Jeanette – and he realised that he did not in fact know where she lived. Perhaps, though, she had thought quite sensibly that keeping a low profile for a couple of weeks they should avoid unnecessary contact. So he decided to drop her a confirmatory message to that effect, but discovered that her Facebook account was now deactivated.

Jeanette Townley was now no more than a name and a grey silhouette, but Nigel wished hopelessly that she could somehow reassure him that their trip to Wales was all just a fiction before she slipped into complete oblivion. But no, it was real, all too real and he needed to realign and get back on track with his plans.

The thought of her deactivated Facebook account goaded him into confrontation with his own apparently forgotten YouTube channel with its promise of mind-blowing revelations about to alert the world to the hidden corruption of the Fellowship of Gilead. That would have to wait, but not for long.

Nigel Clifford was not going to sink into obscurity with all those losers like brainless Vic Scanlon or Amy the Arab who couldn't make it as a real doctor but had to content herself with handing out flea remedies for pussy cats.

*

* 9 *

Lisa

Chapter 19
A Teddy Bear Comes Home

When Lisa was eighteen she left Throstle and had a little flat in the Ridgeway which wasn't very far away and she kept in touch with all the lovely people at Throstle. They still helped her with all sorts of things, like getting a job in the supermarket which was half way between Throstle and the Ridgeway.

But it was still not time to see what there might be along that shadowed passageway. She thought maybe it would never be time. There were some things that popped out of the shadows from time to time that she thought she could remember or kind of glimpse like trying to look through the spooky mist on a wintery day when you couldn't see across to anything far away except for a few seconds now and again when you would suddenly spot something and you knew what it was but then it would be gone and it would be quiet and there was nothing there. That's how it was when she tried to remember where she was before Throstle except that it was the close-up things she couldn't recognise through the mist. Not the far away things which she knew but didn't want to.

What she remembered from just behind one of the big doors in the high wall – and then forgot again right away – was a horse. A man and a girl were riding the horse through the sky but then it would be gone, back into the shadows and hidden behind the big wall.

One day she went back to Throstle. They had told her that Wendy was leaving and some people were putting on a party for her and Lisa wanted to go because Wendy was lovely and kind and everybody liked Wendy. There were lots of people there. All the doctors and nurses and the receptionists and they were all pleased to see Lisa come in through the big red door like she had done years and years before and Wendy saw her and came to her like she did before and gave her a hug but it was Lisa's turn to give Wendy a hug.

Lots of the people she used to know were there including Frank, the counsellor, who had gently tried to persuade her to see if she could look into the shadows or peep through a door or a window in the big wall and see what was behind it – where she had come from before Throstle. He came over while she was talking with Wendy and they had a nice chat. things like, hello and isn't it nice to see everybody and where are you going to next, Wendy? (She was going to be a senior consultant at the big regional office in Preston.)

Then Frank said to Lisa, "Have you taken a look down that passageway yet?"

"Not properly," Lisa replied. "But I did see something," and she told him about the man and the girl riding a horse through the sky and he seemed to think that was interesting.

"Come and talk to me about it sometime," he said.

She still wasn't quite sure but maybe she would.

He didn't press her, he never did. He waited for her to say something else. One eyebrow slightly raised and his head tilted a little to the side like a puppy waiting for a biscuit.

And Lisa said, "I'd have to tell you about going fence hopping."

He nodded, waited a little while and then touched her upper arm gently and said, "Come and talk to me about it sometime."

On her way back to the Ridgeway she remembered. The travelling fairground. The travelling fairground! The wide open playing fields churned up by fairground lorries and caravans. And the houses where some of the kids from the funfair, and some of the local kids as well, used to go thieving from the houses before the rides and the roundabouts and stalls and the music machines were packed up and hitched up and they all moved on in a big long procession to the next borough. And then she remembered about the cards and things and the necklace and brooch that she had lost and she didn't want to remember anything else. Because there was a big empty muddy field and the vans were not there, they were not there, they had gone, and the cards and things were no good to her because the lady who would buy them had gone and she didn't know who else would buy them or who else would find her somewhere to sleep. So she went back where she got the cards and he found them - the man, he found them when he took her knickers off because that was where she had hidden them, except the teddy bear brooch which she wanted to keep for herself. And that was it.

Except that wasn't all. There was something else as well. A face at one of the windows. A kind, friendly face and he was going to help her. He was going to bring back her teddy bear brooch and they would run away together, maybe ride away into the sky on that flying horse. But he never came and there was nothing else. Her memory was empty again, she lost it just like she lost the brooch and there was only that long dark passageway and she couldn't see where it led or where it had come from or what was behind those dark doors and windows.

So on Thursday she went back to Throstle's Nest House and waited to see Frank and when he came out of the office she said she needed to see into the shadows and he said he would help her and he would make it safe. And he did. But there was a lot of crying and hurting along the way and she was sorry that Wendy had gone to Preston.

Lisa had always kept in touch with Wendy because she was more than her counsellor and social worker. She thought of her as a friend – the very first real friend she had ever had even though she was a grown up while Lisa was still only a kid. She always sent her a birthday card and she was the only person who had ever done that. Then one day, years and years after Lisa had moved into her little flat in the Ridgeway, she got a very special message that came to her on her mobile phone.

"Hi," she said when Lisa phoned her back. "I've heard from a couple of people who seem to know some things that we might find interesting, you and me. Now, look, you don't have to meet them if you'd rather not. But they might have some information that could help you take a good look down that long dark passageway and behind its doors and windows. So what I thought is that I could listen to what they have to say and then you can decide whether you'd like to meet them. Are you okay with that?"

Sure she was okay with it. So what they decided was that Wendy could arrange to meet them at Throstle's Nest House some time. And if Lisa was still happy to talk with them, Wendy would be there to support her.

And then the day came. Lisa waited for a few minutes in the big room with the little tables and the chairs where Wendy had brought her on that day years and years before when first she had arrived at Throstle's Nest House. She liked coming back here because it was the place where, for the first time ever in her life, she was able to stop feeling scared and nervous all the time. Right now, though, she did feel a little bit nervous because she was waiting to meet people who used to belong to that time when everything was horrible.

Wendy was in the small room talking with them because, although she had spoken with them already, that was only ever on the phone and she just wanted to chat and sort of finish off getting to know them. And then she came into the big room.

"Hi, Lisa," she said cheerfully like she always does. "Do you want to come with me and meet Amy and Vic? I think they are lovely people and I'm sure you are going to like them."

She went with Wendy to the little room a bit further down the corridor. Her two visitors were sitting beside the window and Lisa could hardly take her eyes off Amy. She had lovely brown eyes that sparkled and smiled and her big soft yellow headscarf gleamed in the sunlight streaming through the window. It was like she was a jewel wrapped in gold and Lisa made up her mind right then that she too was going to look just like that and she was going to get one of those headscarves and wear it like that and be beautiful.

"...and here are Vic and Amy," Wendy was saying. "Now, Vic, would you like to tell Lisa what you have been telling me?"

She listened avidly as he told her how he and his friend used to go on what they called a "snoopers' hunt" which was a bit like how she and the other kids would go stealing things which Queenie, the lady in the big posh caravan at the travelling fairground, would buy from them. But Vic and his friend never actually stole anything which was a bit weird really. Made it all rather pointless, Lisa thought.

"And you never took anything? Nothing at all?"

"There was one thing," he replied and reached for something in his pocket. "When I went back there a few days later to make sure that I really had seen someone in there, I found this lying on the ground in his lean-to and I kept it as sort of proof that you were real. Because it was not what I thought Robinson would have. So I wonder if you might remember it?" He handed her something in a little packet.

Carefully she opened the packet. It was the brooch! The teddy bear brooch she had found in the grass at the feet of the crowds hurrying to the funfair, and then had lost. The brooch she was going to keep for herself because it would be the only nice thing she had. "And you kept it!" she said excitedly. "You kept it for me! You're the face at the window. And you've come back like you promised you would. Oh wow!"

"I had no way to give it back to you until now."

Suddenly she felt unsure. "Do I have to…? I don't don't know whose it could be. There were so many people." She looked at Wendy hoping for some sort of support.

"I don't think there would be any way now to find where it came from before you found it," said Vic. "I think it has to stay with you now, if you want it."

"Yes! Yes I do want it." She stroked the shiny smooth enamel with her finger. She looked up and smiled a deep happy smile at Vic. And then she smoothed the brooch to and fro just a little bit across her cheek. "Thank you, thank you, ever so much." And she gave her big deep thank you smile to each of her three friends, and she felt like a little child who had just been given something really precious that she so much wanted and she ran across the room to Vic and threw her arms around him.

"He spoke to me," she said, looking directly at the teddy bear brooch. "When I found him it was like he spoke to me and said, all the horrible stuff will soon be over and he said it was time for me to start being happy. And then I lost him and I was so sad."

The four of them sat quietly together, Lisa and Wendy and Amy and Vic. Not saying a word. And then Lisa said, "You kept him for me and I am so happy. And he brought you to me. And now… Oh gosh… I can… I can, I really can…" There were tears in her eyes, but they were happy tears.

She looked straight at Vic, then at Amy, like she was trying to give them a hug with her eyes. And she looked at Wendy and said, "I can see it all now. Everything inside those doors and windows and behind the shadows and it doesn't have to be in little bits that make me unhappy and push them away and never see where they fit together and never be able to say what happened to me or where I came from. Or anything."

"And you want to tell us?" suggested Wendy tentatively.

"Yes, I do," Lisa replied.

*

Chapter 20
Into the Shadows

Lisa loved her mum, really she did and her mum loved her but she was a bit of a dilly-o and could never get anything right. And she never knew how to be a mum. By the time she was eight years old Lisa knew that she did not want be the same as her when she grew up.

Her real name was Dorothy but she had to be Colette when she was working because Dorothy wasn't a proper name for a prostitute. They lived with Jacko her pimp who was vile and made her sister Hazel do absolutely revolting things. But Hazel, being stupid, liked it. Well, let her like it but Lisa wanted to get out of it as soon as possible before Jacko could turn on her and get her to "warm up" her mum's customers like Hazel had to while they were waiting their turn.

If she'd had a choice about the way out of all that dark and horrible life she would not have chosen what actually happened, no way, but never mind, it did mean she never had to go back there even though it also meant she lost all contact with her mum. So, what happened was that Jacko got her mum started on the heroin dealing thing. All good clean stuff, he reckoned, and maybe it was at first but then he got a batch that had not been properly cut. It was pure lethal stuff.

And, of course, what happened? One of her mum's crackhead customers comes round, gets warmed up with Hazel and then snorts a load of the graveyard batch when he was already high and that was it, lights out, he drops dead even before he can screw their mum.

Their mum completely lost it and went into a blind panic when she realised what had happened. "What the fuck do I do now?" she screamed over and over. "I wish it was Jacko lying there. Then maybe we'd get a bit of calm and no constant aggro. What the fuck will he do when he sees this?"

Then she turned on Hazel and started screaming at her. "Get out of it! Just don't be around when he comes back. He'll be pissed out of his skull. Hazel, will you get out, for fuck's sake and take the kid with you! Just don't be here."

So Lisa and Hazel ran off into the night and huddled together underneath the stairs in the shopping centre. They managed to dodge the security staff on their locking-up routine and then went home when the centre opened in the morning.

All was calm when they got back home. Their mum was still sleeping and Jacko was nowhere around. And there was no sign of the unfortunate customer. "What happened?" Hazel asked when their mum came downstairs.

No reply. She put the kettle on and dropped onto the sofa. "Make us a cuppa, Hazel, love."

The girls sat with their mum while she sipped her coffee and waited for her to say something. "I'm sorry, girls. Truly I am," she said at last. "I've fucked up good and proper this time. And I'm so sorry. I'll make it up to you. Fuck knows how, but I will. I promise."

It meant that the girls had to leg it because the police would be sure to be on their way and if they were still around then, they'd be taken into care, that's for certain. Their mum reckoned once the police knew all the details she'd be able to come home. There would be a trial, of course, but she would probably get off with a suspended sentence or no more than a couple of years at the most because, after all, it was Jacko's fault not hers. She was innocent really.

So the girls had to be out of the way until it had all blown over. They each stuffed some clothes and things into a bag and headed off towards the A1. They hitched a lift south, well several actually because they had to leg it a couple of times to get away from gropey drivers. But they managed to get as far as Leeds which Hazel reckoned was as good as anywhere and after a few nights of sheltering in shop doorways they found a pretty good squat in an old pub where half a dozen or more other youngsters and grown-ups lived and shared end-of-the-day throw-aways from supermarkets and stuff they were able to nick or beg.

It could have been good if it hadn't been for Ronnie who started trying to persuade a couple of the girls, including Hazel, to go on the game. Hazel thought it was a great idea but Lisa didn't. She could only think that Ronnie was another Jacko in the making. So she legged it again.

She ran and kept on running for ages and ages and came to a wide open field. There were lorries and huge trailers and big posh caravans with lacy net curtains at the windows. There were lots of men shouting to each other and loading stuff that looked like fairground things onto the trailers. There was rubbish all over the place and people walking up and down gathering it all up into bags. And Lisa saw a way to escape.

She tossed her bag into one of the fully loaded trailers then climbed in and tucked herself underneath the tarpaulin. They would start to move soon, she knew it. She would go with them, never mind where that might be. And she would escape. She would be free and maybe at long last she would be able to be an ordinary girl and perhaps even go to school and learn to read and write and know what it said in books and letters and on boards and signs, without having to ask her sister.

Someone came along just outside where she was in the trailer and began to fasten the tarpaulin down firmly. A little while later they started to move. She could feel it bumping slowly over the rough field. She lurched against whatever it was she had been leaning against. A horse, like a big rocking horse with shiny big teeth and a gaily coloured face. She looked into the horse's eyes and he smiled at her. "We're off on a new adventure now," the horse seemed to say.

The journey took forever until at last the backing and lurching and manoeuvring suggested they had reached the end. Lisa managed to lift a corner of the tarpaulin and peep out from underneath. They appeared to be on some big lorry park like the one along the A1 where she'd had to leg it to get away from a gropey driver. And it was mostly lorries, not many fairground trailers or caravans like she would have expected. She crawled across to the other side of the trailer and peeped out from there. Yes, there were a few of them but it wasn't the whole lot.

As she was trying to work out what was going on a man came along checking the trailer and he caught her before she could hide. He unfastened a part of the tarp as she cowered in the gloom.

"And who do you think you are, young lady?" he asked, but he sounded more friendly than angry.

"I was just... Well, I was trying to get... Don't know."

"You don't know where you are going? Is that it?"

She was feeling really scared. Between gasps, she blurted out, "My mum's gone to prison... And I ran away with my sister... But she's a prostie like my mum... And I don't want to..."

"So you're running away but you don't know where?"

"Yes."

He began to unfasten more of the tarp. "Right then, young lady. Out you get and we'll see what we can do for you." He took her bag and then helped her down from the trailer. "First, get cleaned up, eh?"

She went with him across to the far side of the lorry park where there was a toilet and shower block. He punched a code into the key pad. "In you go. You got clean clothes in here?" he asked holding up her bag.

She nodded.

"Okay. Get yourself showered. There's plenty of paper towels in there. And then bundle up those things you're wearing and we'll get it all washed for you. Okay? I'll wait for you out here."

She felt lots better when she came out because that was the first proper wash she'd had since running away from home. She felt fresh and nice and not so scared and the man smiled at her like he was really going to be a friend.

"Okay, then," he said. "Let's take you over to Queenie. I'm sure she'll have a place for you on her team."

Queenie's caravan was a big posh thing but nothing like as grand as some of those mobile palaces there had been on the huge fairground. Queenie was the mum and the granny and the boss of the small travelling funfair and she would fix up for them to join other fairgrounds or to do simple market place funfairs in small towns all over the place. She had huge rings on every finger, thick make-up that looked like it could even be a mask and a pinky blonde hairdo that looked like she bought it in a posh hat shop. But she wasn't scary. She had a lovely friendly smile and, yes, she thought she could find a place for Lisa on her team.

It looked like it was going to be good. Queenie got one of the men to find an inflatable bed and some blankets for Lisa and they let her sleep in the back of one of the big vans and then when they went to join a big travelling funfair the team would get her working with them getting the stuff that Queenie wanted.

It was simple really, one of the other girls told her as they arrived at the fairground in goodness knows where. Basically two things – either pockets or bag dipping among the crowds, or else fence hopping and rooting about in the houses near the fairground. And what Queenie needed were bank cards, driving licences, jewellery. It was usual, apparently, to start off working the crowds (and always be ready to run) and then to switch to fence hopping when it was coming near time for the funfair to move on.

She had a couple of days on bag dipping and that wasn't too difficult because while she was just learning another girl did the actual dipping and what Lisa had to do was be ready all the time to quickly grab whatever the other girl handed her and stuff it out of sight in her own pockets. Then if the dipper was ever challenged she would able to say that, look, no she didn't have anything at all that she'd snatched. So it was dip, handover, hide and always be ready to just wander off casually while the dipper girl made a run for cover. Easy.

Fence hopping was much more tricky but along by the field where the fairground was there were lots of houses that were the easiest sort. They had all sorts of sheds and things built on and jutting out bits and passageways and corners so it was really quite easy to keep out of sight once you had climbed over the fence.

Lisa got lucky at the first house she tried. She went over the fence and round the edge of the overgrown garden. Then, carefully and quietly and keeping low down, she went around the back of the house, listening just by windows. No sounds from inside. Down the side of the house listening at more windows. Peeping out to the front of the house. No cars out there. Then very carefully, very very carefully, trying a door handle. Locked. Trying to peep through windows, sometimes needing find something to stand on. No sign of anyone. Trying to open a window. Locked. Locked. Locked. Open! A second careful peep inside. Nobody.

She opened the window fully and waited a few moments. Nobody. She pulled herself up at the open window and got a better look inside. Clear! She climbed through and she was there! She had done it! She was in the house.

It looked like an ordinary slightly untidy sitting room. Keeping her eye on where the open window was just in case she needed to get out in a hurry, she went around the room, checking in drawers, looking in vases and behind clocks. Nothing worth taking.

She cautiously opened the door very slightly and looked through to what appeared to be the entrance hall. She listened for a few moments. No sounds. She went through, leaving the door wide open in case she needed an emergency get-out. Up near the front door there was a stand with some coats hanging on it. In the middle of it there was a mirror with a little shelf and a drawer and a telephone and on the top was a brass box.

She looked in the drawer. A couple of hairbrushes and a hand mirror. She opened the box. Some tie-pins and cuff-links. And lucky! A necklace! A beautiful glassy blue jewel with lots of little jewels around it. Lisa knew it was silver because of the little markings on the lacy metalwork of the pendant, and the chain was of the same stuff. It was a good one. She was sure it was a good one. So she put it into her pocket and quietly and carefully went back out of the house through the same window where she came in. And just to make sure that nobody would immediately think anything was amiss when they got back home, she pushed the window shut before creeping away to the back fence.

She jogged happily back towards the fairground and imagined how pleased Queenie would be with the lovely necklace which she had found. As she came closer she met one of the others, a girl a little older and skinnier and scruffier than the rest of Queenie's team. "You look pleased with yourself," the girl said.

"Yes," said Lisa brightly. "Look what I got!" She reached into her pocket, pulled out the necklace and held it up for the other girl to admire.

"Is that it? A crappy little thing like that! For fuck's sake, kiddo, you've got to do better than that. Cause, believe me, fence hopping is far better than any of the other jobs Queenie can make you do."

The girl ran on and Lisa watched as she was swallowed up into the motor-driven gaiety of the fairground's flashing lights and noisy music. She turned and looked back towards the long row of houses at the edge of the park. Right at that moment the late afternoon's lengthening shadows of the grim old houses was far less unappealing than the prospect of discovering what alternative work Queenie might find for a failed fence-hopper.

She knelt down in a huddle on the grass and tried not to cry. And glistening as if it was calling to her, she spotted something in the grass. A shiny teddy bear brooch and it seemed to be telling her she was going to be okay. She picked it up, fingered it gently and put it into her shirt pocket. She stood up and told herself not to give up.

As she looked at that long row of houses from a hundred yards or so away, she noticed a narrow passageway that seemed to lead out of the park. She headed towards it and went down between the houses to the road. Her first instinct was to keep back out of sight but then she decided to go out onto the road and walk up and down the fronts of those forbidding houses, counting carefully from the passageway as she went. Number one, no car at the front and no open windows. Number two, wide open windows and a car at the front. And so on.

Number one, beside the passageway looked promising. She went back into the park and along number one's back fence. There was a place she could get over quite easily so, taking care to check that there was nobody around to see her, she went over the fence and followed the same routine as before checking and double checking that there was nobody at home.

This one was much easier than the first. There was a sort of extension thing at the back with no upstairs part to it. And in the corner between the extension and the back wall of the house there were a few steps up to the back door which had another door beside it that looked like it went into the extension. On the end of the extension there was a rickety old shed.

And then, on the other side of the back door was a window which was quite high up looking like the floor inside was the same height as the top of the steps up to the back door. Well, of course it would be. That meant it wasn't easy to look into the house and like the other one she would have to find something to climb up onto. But, never mind, because the window was actually open, wide open and she was sure there was nobody inside.

It was a bit of a squeeze but she got through and found herself in the kitchen. She peeped and listened at the door and then, confident that there was nobody around, she began to explore. A very big sitting room yielded nothing of any interest.

The next room was different, much smaller, with bookshelves and cabinets and a cluttered up desk. In fact everywhere was cluttered with books and papers lying around all over the place. She rooted among the papers scattered on the desk. And then got lucky! Underneath the papers and just lying there, were two bank cards and a driving licence. She stuffed them into her pocket and began to look in the drawers. Nothing of very much interest. Except, wait, right at the back of the top drawer there was a passport. And she knew that her findings here were things that Queenie would be able to use.

She didn't hear him coming back until it was too late. She heard his key in the front door and saw his shadowed figure against the coloured glass. Quickly she ran back to the kitchen and its open window but she had only squeezed her head and shoulders through when she felt his hands firmly grasping her ankles. He pulled her back into the kitchen and stood, menacingly it seemed, over her.

She could hardly speak. Just, "No," to everything, whatever it was he was saying or demanding of her. No. No, no no no. Jacko would have thrashed and punched her, her mum would have screamed and shouted and slapped her. But this guy, frightening though he was, was a little bit different. She could tell he wasn't going to hit her. He was angry but he didn't shout.

He said something about taking her to the police and for a moment she thought maybe they might actually help her. But no, of course not. That was silly because they would find those bank cards and things which she still had in her pocket. And then she realised the man was going to find them very soon. At the first chance she thought she might do it without him noticing, she took them from her pocket and, keeping them out of sight, pushed them down inside the waistband of her jeans and into her knickers.

He took her to the back door and told her to go away. Slowly she walked down the garden. She glanced back and saw him standing there in the doorway, making sure that she went away. She climbed over the fence and headed towards to fairground as it sang and danced and whirled its way towards the end of its final day. The disdainful tones of the other girl sneered in her head. That necklace? Rubbish, you'll have to do better than that. Those few cards and things she had found, would they be enough? Or were they rubbish too? Would she still need to do better? But she couldn't. She knew she could never do better.

She turned and slouched miserably back to that gap in the hedge. Maybe she could... What if she could snuggle down in a corner of that man's crappy shed...? And if she could find a way to put those cards back... Would he let her stay in his shed until she could think of something? Would he even help her? She climbed over his fence and sank back into his shadows.

*

* 10 *

Vic and Lisa

Chapter 21
Out of the Darkness

Just a few short weeks. That's all it had been since Amy's first Facebook message that started the process of piecing this story together. And how much had happened in the time since then! It was fortunate that they'd had time to contact Wendy Davidson with the awful crazy news from Wales of Robbo dead for several days in his isolated cottage and Nigel arrested for his part in the bloody affair. And this Jeanette Townley, who was she? Was that her real name? Where was she? Would they ever find her?

Fortunate though, that Wendy could forewarn Lisa so that the news would not have to come along with her visit to Colinton. Vic wanted to make her visit special and not simply the grim reminder of the place where horrible things happened to her. And perhaps it could be special and he could be cautiously buoyant about the prospect of enjoying a couple of days in her company.

He waited on the platform as her train rolled in, smoothly and massively as the sound of its great engines merged with the hum of the busy station, rendering the locomotive weirdly silent. There was a pause after it had come to a halt and then the carriage doors all slid open and passengers poured out onto the platform. And there she was, near the head of the hurrying procession as if leading it with a skip in her step when she spotted Vic.

She ran up to him, dropped her bag at his feet and threw her arms around him. “Vic! I am so pleased to see you!”

Oh wow! This was far more and far better than he had hoped. From the scared kid huddled in a shadowed corner, to a nervous young woman, protege of the lovely and very special Dr Wendy, and now this lively girl on an adventure. He’d scarcely allowed himself to even think it. But he couldn’t help remembering that crazy schoolboy fantasy when he’d imagined himself rescuing her from Robbo’s prison cell and they would live together in his grandad’s old tent in a hidden corner of Kenwood Park.

But no, this was Lisa’s day, hers alone to find out at last where it had happened for she had never found out where she was back then. It was a time for her to lay some ghosts forever and Vic was there simply as a guide and no more.

They drove to the park and came onto the playing fields at the top end furthest from where Robbo’s place had been. They stood side by side and looked in silence across the wide open space. There was just one other person, a woman throwing a ball for her dog to chase. Vic and Lisa walked slowly across the field and stopped halfway. Lisa dropped to her knees and felt the moist grass.

“It was here,” she said. “Oh gosh, just somewhere near here. It’s where I found him. My teddy bear.” She stood up and and unzipped her jacket. “And here he is,” she said showing the brooch pinned to her jumper. “I’m going to get it altered. Get the pin taken off and a loop put there so I can have it on a necklace. Then I can wear it all the time.”

They walked on a little way and stopped again as they came closer to the new flats and houses at the edge of the park. “They’ve gone,” she said. “The fairground with its bright lights that you can’t look into. And that horrid house and its shadows. Gone” She stood a little closer, almost leaning on him. “But you’re here. You said you’d come back and help me. And you’re here.”

“Yes, I’m here.”

“And you won’t go away? You’ll always be here?”

“I’ll always be here.”

“Hold me.”

He put his arms around her. It was too soon to say what he wanted to say. He kissed her instead. For now he would just gently show her what he meant. The words would follow. For now a kiss would say it all.

the end

*

Other Novels by Robert Crompton

Solomon's Magpie

With *Solomon's Magpie* Robert Crompton returned to his favourite haunts in Cheshire to disentangle a story told by Solomon Whitaker, boatman, basket-maker and brewer. Solomon heard the tale from his mother and he went to the trouble of learning to read and write so that he could set it down.

Generations later, fifteen-year-old Judy must try to create a readable version of the story. But there's a problem – a large portion of it is missing, and it is clearly the most important bit. Supported by her unlikely friendships with Twirl and Tracey, Judy fills in the gaps herself. Nobody believes her, however, because she is a compulsive spinner of yarns and teller of tall tales.

Nobody will be sure what happened unless the missing pages are found – and with them Solomon's magpie.

*

Find **Solomon's Magpie** on Amazon

Leaving Gilead

When young Tom Sparrow falls in love with Susan Ridley his dad insists that no good will come of it. Her family belongs to a strict religious sect and they disapprove of all outsiders. Against the odds their friendship develops until the time when Tom is all set to go to university and Susan is free at last to escape from her family's religion and move to Manchester with Tom. What stopped her? Why was she no longer around?

Thirty years later when he is contemplating a change of career, the Ridley's old house, tucked away in the forest, comes up for sale. It is just what he wants – though he isn't sure about Melanie, a young woman who also has an interest in the house. Otherwise it is perfect for his plans for a new life back where he has his roots. As he prepares to move in he discovers something hidden away in an outbuilding and at last he begins to learn the truth of what happened all those years before.

Leaving Gilead is the story of two women's struggles to build new lives after growing up in a religion that promotes irrational belief and conformity with arbitrary rules above personal development.

*

Find **Leaving Gilead** on Amazon

Bunderlin

The story of a simple man, living his life by his own rules and the havoc that he plays in the lives of other people, who cannot seem to disentangle themselves from him. Bunderlin may be a criminal, a murderer even, but Martin isn't sure…

Bunderlin, Bundy, Bird, The Big Man—even his name becomes wordplay. An irresistible force in the lives of the people he decides will be his friends. Bunderlin is infuriating, charming and often plain rude. He enters Martin's life in a sinister way—Martin is being followed, he receives photographs anonymously, he is suddenly thrown from his comfortable life in academia into the social world of hookers, petty criminals and murderers. But could Bunderlin, a man obsessed with kindness to animals, in fact be a killer himself?

Idiosyncratic use of language is a hallmark of Bunderlin's character, and also of this book; a novel that is a delightful and absorbing read. Robert Crompton has constructed a story full of characters who defy stereotype and worm their way into your affections.

*

Find **Bunderlin** on Amazon

Printed in Great Britain
by Amazon

53791734R00133